it would
be night in
caracas

it would
be night in
caracas

a novel

KARINA SAINZ BORGO

Translated from the Spanish by Elizabeth Bryer

HARPERVIA

An Imprint of HarperCollinsPublishers

IT WOULD BE NIGHT IN CARACAS

Original Spanish language publication:
Copyright © 2019 by Karina Sainz Borgo.

English translation:
Copyright © 2019 by Elizabeth Bryer.

Originally published as *La hija de la española* in Spain in 2019 by Lumen.

FIRST HARPERCOLLINS PAPERBACK EDITION PUBLISHED IN 2020

Designed by SBI Book Arts, LLC

Library of Congress Cataloging-in-Publication Data is available upon request.

ISBN 978-0-06-293685-1

20 21 22 23 24   LSC   10 9 8 7 6 5 4 3 2 1

To the women and men who came before me.
And to those who will come after.

Because all stories about the ocean are
political, and each of us
is searching for a land to call home.

Ay, nothing can intimidate you, poet,
Not even the wind in the wires. . . .
Lift your head
But may the words you write
Make sense.

—YOLANDA PANTIN,
  "The Pelvic Bone"

They willed me bravery. I wasn't brave.

—JORGE LUIS BORGES,
  "Remorse"
  translated by Willis Barnstone

I too was reared, like thee, in exile.

—SOPHOCLES
  translated by F. Storr

it would
be night in
caracas

WE BURIED MY MOTHER with her things: her blue dress, her black flats, and her multifocals. We couldn't say good-bye in any other way, couldn't take those things from her. It would have been like returning her to the earth incomplete. We buried it all, because after her death we were left with nothing. Not even each other. That day we were struck down with exhaustion. She in her wooden box; I on a chair in the dilapidated chapel, the only one available of the five or six I tried for the wake. I could hire it for only three hours. Instead of funeral parlors, the city now had furnaces. People went in and out like loaves of bread, which were in short supply on the shelves but rained down in our memory whenever hunger overcame us.

If I still say "we" when I talk about that day it's out of habit, for the years welded us together like two parts of a sword we could use to defend each other. Writing out the inscription for her headstone, I understood that death takes place in language first, in that act of wrenching subjects from the present and planting them in the past. Completed actions. Things that had a beginning and an end, in a time that's gone forever. What was but would never be again. That was the way things were now: from then on, my mother would exist only if worded differently. Burying her meant my life as a childless daughter came to an end. In a city in its death throes, we had lost everything, even words conjugated in the present.

Six people attended my mother's wake. Ana was the first. She arrived dragging her feet. Julio, her husband, was supporting her by the arm. Ana seemed to be moving through a dark tunnel that disgorged her into the world where the rest of us lived. For months, she had been undergoing treatment with benzodiazepine. Its effects were starting to evaporate. Barely enough pills were left to complete her daily dose. As had happened with the bread, there were Alprazolam shortages, which meant despair prevailed, as potent as our desperation. We could only watch as everything we needed vanished: people, places, friends, recollections, food, serenity, peace, sanity. "Lose" became a leveling verb, and the Sons of the Revolution wielded it against us.

Ana and I met in the Department of Humanities. Since then, Ana's life and my own were in sync when it came to going through private hells. This time was no exception. When my mother went into the palliative care facility, the Sons of the Revolution arrested Santiago, Ana's brother. Dozens of students were apprehended that day. They ended up with their backs red raw from the pellets, bludgeoned in a corner, or raped with the barrel of a gun. Santiago got the La Tumba treatment—a combination of all three.

He spent more than a month inside the prison, which extended five floors belowground. Sounds were muffled and there were no windows, no natural light, and no ventilation. The only noises were the screech and clatter of the metro rails above. Santiago was locked inside one of the seven cells. They were aligned one behind the other, so he couldn't see who else was detained. Each cell measured two by three meters. The floor and walls were white. So were the beds and the bars through which his jailers pushed trays of food. It never came with cutlery; if he wanted to eat, he had to do so with his hands.

For several weeks there had been no word from him. Ana wasn't even getting the calls she paid periodic sums of money for any longer, or the faulty proof of life she received previously in the form of photos sent from a different phone number each time.

We don't know if he's alive or dead. "We've had no news," Julio said in a low voice, moving away from the chair where Ana spent thirty minutes staring at her feet. The whole time, she only raised her head to ask three questions.

"What time will Adelaida be buried?"

"At two thirty."

"Okay," she murmured. "Where?"

"In La Guarita cemetery, the old part. My mother bought a plot a long time ago. It has a nice view."

"Okay . . ." Ana seemed to be making an effort, as if processing my words were a titanic task. "Do you want to stay with us today, until the worst of it is over?"

"I'm leaving for Ocumare early tomorrow to go see my aunts. I've got to give them a few things," I lied. "But thank you. This is a difficult time for you too, I know."

"Okay." Ana gave me a kiss on the cheek and left. Who wants to attend a funeral when you can sense your own brother's fast approaching?

Next to arrive were María Jesús and Florencia, retired teachers my mother had kept in touch with over the years. They expressed their condolences and left quickly, conscious that nothing they could say or do would make up for the death of a woman too young to be taken from us. They left at a clip, as if trying to get a head start on the reaper, before he came for them too. Not a single wreath of flowers arrived at the funeral parlor except my own, an arrangement of white carnations that barely covered the upper half of the casket.

My mother's two sisters, my twin aunts Amelia and Clara, weren't present either. One was rotund, and the other was painfully thin. One ate without stopping, while all the other had for breakfast was a small portion of black beans, while she sucked on a roll-your-own cigarette. They lived in Ocumare de la Costa, a town in the state of Aragua, near Bahía de Cata and Choroní. A place where azure waters lapped at white sand, cut off from Caracas by crumbling roads that were becoming impassable.

At eighty years of age, my aunts had made at most a single trip to Caracas. They didn't leave their sleepy backwater even to attend my mother's graduation, and she'd been the first university graduate in the Falcón family. She looked stunning in the photos, standing in the Aula Magna of the Central University of Venezuela: heavy makeup around her eyes, her teased hair squashed flat beneath the mortarboard, the certificate in her rigid hands, and a smile that looked lonely, like she was quietly furious. My mother kept that photograph alongside her Bachelor of Education academic transcript and the notice that my aunts had placed in *El Aragüeño*, the regional newspaper, so that everyone would know that the Falcóns now had a professional in the family.

We didn't see my aunts often, only once or twice a year. We traveled to the small town where they lived in July and August, sometimes during Carnaval or Semana Santa. We would give them a hand with the guesthouse and help lighten their financial load. My mother always left them a little money, pestering them while she was at it: one to stop eating, the other to eat. They lavished us with breakfasts that turned my stomach: shredded beef, crispy pork rind, tomato, avocado, and *guarapo*, a beverage made of cinnamon and unrefined sugar strained through a cloth. They often followed me around the house brandishing the brew, which more than a few times made me faint; I would regain consciousness to the sounds of their fussing.

"Adelaida, if our mother saw this girl of yours, puny as she is and with no meat on her bones, she'd dish her up three arepas smothered in lard," my aunt Amelia, the rotund one, would say. "What do you do to the poor creature? She's no bigger than a fried herring. Wait here, m'hija. I'll be right back. . . . Don't you move a muscle, muchachita!"

"Leave the girl in peace, Amelia. Just because you're hungry all the time doesn't mean everyone else is," my aunt Clara would sing out from the patio, keeping an eye on her mango trees and smoking a cigarette.

"Aunt Clara, what are you doing out there? Come inside, we're about to eat."

"Hold on, I want to make sure those scoundrels from next door don't come knock down any of my mangoes with a rod. The other day they took three bags' worth."

"Here you go, eat only one if you want but there are three more," said my aunt Amelia, back from the kitchen, with a plate of fried bollos stuffed with pork picadillo. "Come on, eat up, m'hija, it's getting cold!"

After doing the washing up, the three women would sit on the patio to play bingo amid the clouds of mosquitoes that descended at six in the evening, the same time every day. We always scared them off with the smoke that rose from the dry brushwood once it caught alight. We would make a bonfire and would draw together to watch it burn beneath the day's dying sun. Then one of the twins, sometimes Clara and sometimes Amelia, would turn in her rattan chair and, growling, would say the magic words: the Dead One.

That was how they referred to my father, an engineering student whose plans to marry my mother were wiped from his mind when she told him she was expecting. Judging by the anger my aunts radiated, anyone would say they'd been left in the lurch too. They mentioned him much more than my mother did; I never heard her speak his name. No word came from him after he left, or so my mother told me. It seemed a good enough incentive not to be fazed by his absence. If he didn't want to hear from us, then why should we expect anything from him?

I never understood our family to be a large one. Family

meant the two of us, my mother and me. Our family tree started and ended with us. Together we formed a junco, a plant capable of growing anywhere. We were small and veiny, almost ribbed, perhaps so it wouldn't hurt if a piece of us was wrenched off, or even if we were pulled out by the roots. We were made to endure. Our world was sustained by the two of us keeping it in balance. Everything outside our family of two was the exception: supplementary, and for that reason expendable. We weren't waiting on anyone; we had each other and that was enough.

U TTER DESTRUCTION. That was the feeling I had as I dialed the Falcón guesthouse the day of my mother's wake. My aunts took their time answering the phone. Two ailing women in that big old house, they had trouble making it from the patio to the lounge room, where a small coin-operated telephone was still connected even though nobody used it anymore. They'd run the guesthouse for thirty years. That whole time they'd changed not even a painting. They were like that, as improbable as the rosy trumpet trees painted on dusty canvases that decorated the grease- and dirt-covered walls.

After several failed attempts, they finally picked up. They took the news of my mother's death in a bleak mood, saying little. First, I spoke to Clara, the skinny one, then to Amelia, the rotund one. They ordered me to postpone the burial for at least the time it would take them to catch the next bus to Caracas. Between them and the capital was a three-hour journey on a road riddled with potholes and thugs. Those conditions, on top of their old age and ill health—one had diabetes, the other arthritis—would have broken them down. Those seemed reasons enough to dissuade them from coming. I said good-bye, promising to come see them soon—I was lying—so we could say a novena in the town chapel. They conceded reluctantly. I hung up the phone sure of one thing: the world as I knew it had begun to unravel.

Toward midday, two neighbors from our building appeared, expressing their condolences and letting loose a barrage of consolations, as useless as tossing bread to pigeons. María, a nurse who lived on the sixth floor, went on about eternal life. Gloria from the penthouse seemed more interested in knowing what would become of me now that I was "all alone." Of course, the apartment was too large for a childless woman. Of course, the way things were, I'd have to consider renting out at least one of the rooms. Today you get paid in US dollars, Gloria said, if you're lucky enough to find someone you know. Respectable people, good pay. There are so many crooks around. And since solitude does nobody any good, and now you're all on your own, it would be wise to have others around, wouldn't it, at least in case of an emergency. You must know someone to rent out a room to, do you? I expect you do, but if not, I have a distant cousin who right this minute is looking for a place to rent in the city. What a fabulous opportunity, don't you think? She could move in with you, and you could earn a little extra. A great idea, no?

She spilled these words over the closed casket of my still-warm mother.

Because, as you no doubt saw, paying the doctors, and the funeral, and the cemetery plot with the inflation as it is. . . .

Because no doubt all this cost you a fortune, didn't it? I'm sure you still have some money saved up, but with your aunts being so elderly and so far away, you'll need another source of income. I'll put you in touch with my cousin, so you can put that room to good use.

Gloria didn't stop talking about money for an instant. Something in her little rodent eyes told me she would make off with whatever there was to take from my situation or would at least improve her own circumstances by leveraging mine. That's the way we were all living: peering at what was in each other's shopping bag. Sniffing out when a neighbor came home with something in short supply, so we could investigate where to get hold of it. We were all becoming suspicious and watchful. We would distort solidarity into predation.

The women left after two hours, one sick of hearing the other's indelicacies, the other worn out after failing to discover what would become of my dead mother's estate.

Life had become a matter of venturing out to hunt and returning home alive. That was what our daily activities had turned into, even burying our dead.

"The chapel hire will be five thousand bolívares fuertes."

"You mean five million old bolívares."

"Yes, that's right," the funeral parlor employee raised his soft voice. "Given that you've presented the death certificate, it's cheaper. Otherwise, it would be seven thousand bolívares fuertes, because issuing the certificate incurs an additional fee."

"Seven million old bolívares, was it?"

"Yes, exactly."

"Okay."

"So would you like to hire our services?" He sounded a little exasperated.

"Does it look like I have a choice?"

"Only you know that."

Paying for the wake was even more complicated than paying for my mother's final days in the clinic. The banking system was a fiction. The funeral parlor had no credit card reader, they didn't accept bank transfers, and I didn't have enough cash to cover the quantity requested, which was something like two thousand times my monthly wage. Even if I'd had the cash, they wouldn't have accepted it. No one wanted cash anymore. Cash was worthless bits of paper. You needed several wads to buy anything—from a bottle of soda, if you could find one, to a small pack of chewing gum, which might cost ten or twelve times what it was originally worth. Money had taken on an urban scale. Two towers of hundred-bolívar bills were needed for a bottle of cooking oil; sometimes it took three to buy a quarter kilo of cheese. Worthless skyscrapers, that's what our national currency had become: a tall tale. A few months later, the opposite happened: all the money disappeared. This meant we had nothing to exchange for the little we could still find.

I opted for the simplest solution. I took out my last fifty-euro note, which I'd bought months before on the black market, and handed it to the funeral director, who pounced on it, his eyes lit with astonishment. He would probably exchange it for twenty times its official worth, or even thirty times what I'd paid. Fifty euros, a quarter of what remained of the savings I had wrapped in old undergarments to bamboozle any intruder. A stint for a Mexican publishing house based in Spain—they paid me in foreign currency—and overdue payments for edited manuscripts had meant my mother and I could get by, but the past few weeks had been brutal. The clinic charged for everything they didn't have, and we had to buy it on the black market for three or four times its original worth: from syringes and saline bags to gases and cotton buds. A nurse with the air of a butcher handed over each item after naming an exorbitant price, almost always higher than the one we'd agreed on.

Everything was disappearing as fast as my mother faded. She shared a room with three other patients, lying in a bed made up with the freshly washed sheets I had to bring from home every day, sheets that seemed to soak up the room's sickly air. There wasn't a single clinic that didn't have a waiting list for its beds. People got sick and died as fast as they lost their minds. I never considered subjecting my mother to a public hospital, it would have been like leaving her to die in a cold corridor, stuck between criminals riddled with bullets. Everything was ending: our life, our money, our strength. Even the days were now abbreviated. Being in the street at six in the evening was asking to cut your life short. Anything could kill us: a stray bullet, a kidnapping, a robbery. Blackouts lasted long hours and meant sunsets were followed by everlasting darkness.

At two in the afternoon, funeral parlor employees appeared in the chapel, two strong-looking individuals dressed in dark suits sewn from cheap fabric. They hauled the casket outside and threw it into a Ford Zephyr that had been converted into a hearse. I had to grab the wreath and lay it atop the casket to make it clear that this was my mother, not a platter of mortadella. In a place where death was equated with casualties from a plague, the body of Adelaida Falcón, my mother, was a cold cut, one lifeless body among so many others. The men treated her as they treated everyone else— completely devoid of compassion.

I got into the passenger seat and looked at the driver out of the corner of my eye. He had gray hair and the pitted skin of an aging black man. "Which cemetery are we going to? La Guarita?" I nodded. We said nothing further. The city's hot wind embraced me. It had a sweet-and-sour smell of orange peel rotting inside a plastic bag beneath the sweltering sun. Driving along the motorway took twice as long as usual. In the past fifty years, the city had grown to at least three times the population that the main artery had been designed for.

The Zephyr had no shocks, so the potholed road was an ordeal. With no straps to hold it secure, my mother's casket bounced around in the back. As I looked in the rearview mirror at the veneer box—I hadn't been able to afford a timber one—I thought about how much I would have liked to give my mother a fitting funeral. She must have thought along similar lines all too often. She must have wished to give me better things: a cuter lunch box, like the pink ones with gold trim that my schoolmates bought every October, not the workaday blue plastic one that she washed out thoroughly every September; a bigger house with a garden in the city's east, not our birdcage apartment in the west. I never questioned anything my mother gave me because I knew how much it cost her. How many tutorials she'd had to teach to pay for my private-school education, or for my birthday parties, which were always overflowing with cakes, jelly, and soda served in plastic cups. She never said. Yet where the money came from needed no explaining because I saw it with my own eyes.

My mother had taught private tutorials on Tuesdays, Wednesdays, and Thursdays every week. These turned into daily sessions during the holidays for students who had to take exams in September so as not to fail a course. At a quarter to four, she would remove the tablecloth from the dining table. On its surface she would place pencils, a sharpener, several blank sheets of paper, a plate with María cookies, a jug of water, and two glasses. So many children passed through our house. They all had the same anemic look, no life in them. Overweight and indifferent girls and boys, undernourished thanks to all the chocolate and television that filled their afternoons in a city that was doing away with its parks. I grew up in a place full of rusty slides and swing sets, but everyone was too fearful of crime to play on them, and back then the crime rate wasn't a shadow of what it came to be.

My mother would outline the basics: subject, verb, and predicate, then direct, indirect, and circumstantial complements. There was no way to get it right except to go over it again and again, and sometimes not even that was enough. So many years of correcting exams written in gray lead, preparing morning lessons, and supervising her students with their homework in the evenings meant my mother's sight deteriorated. Toward the end, slipping off her pearly acetate glasses was almost impossible. She could do nothing without them. Even though her daily reading of the paper became slower and more difficult, she never stopped doing it. She thought it was civilized.

Adelaida Falcón was a cultured woman. The library in our house had books from the Circle of Readers monthly subscription service—universal and contemporary classics in electric colors that I consulted thousands of times during my degree and ended up adopting as my own. Those volumes fascinated me even more than the pink lunch boxes that my classmates flaunted every October.

WHEN WE ARRIVED at the cemetery, the gravesite with its two pits had already been dug. One for her, the other for me. My mother had bought the plot years before. Looking at that clay recess, I thought of a Juan Gabriel Vásquez line that I'd seen on a galley I'd proofread a few weeks before: "Each of us belongs to the place where our dead are buried." As I observed the shorn grass around her grave, I understood that my mother, my only dead, tied me to this land. And this land exiled its people as forcefully as it devoured them. This was not a nation. It was a meat mincer.

The cemetery workers removed my mother from the Ford Zephyr and lowered her into the grave with the help of pulleys and old belts full of rivets. At least what had happened to my grandmother Consuelo wouldn't happen to my mother. I was very young, but I remember it to this day. It was in Ocumare. It was hot, a saltier and more humid heat. My tongue had been seared by the guarapo that my aunts forced me to drink between one Ave Maria and another, and I kept worrying at it as the town gravediggers lowered the casket with two frayed ropes. All of a sudden, the casket slid sideways. On impact, it broke open like a pistachio. My stiff

17

grandmother banged against the glass top, and the gathering of loved ones went from intoning the requiem to shrieking. Two young men tried to right her, close the box, and get on with the proceedings, but things got complicated. My aunts paced around the pit, grasping their heads and praying to the top brass of the Catholic Church. San Pedro, San Pablo, Virgen Santísima, Virgen Purísima, Reina de los Ángeles, Reina de los Patriarcas, Reina de los Profetas, Reina de los Apóstoles, Reina de los Mártires, Reina de los Confesores, Reina de las Vírgenes. Pray for us.

My grandmother, an unloving woman at the foot of whose grave some joker planted a hot chili, died in her bed, calling for her eight dead sisters. Eight women dressed in black. She saw them on the other side of the mosquito netting beneath which she was dispensing her final commands. So said my mother, who, by contrast, had no parade of relations to command from her throne with the aid of pillows and spittoons. My mother had only me.

A priest recited from a missal for the soul of Adelaida Falcón, my mother. The workers shoveled the clay and sealed the grave with a cement board, the mezzanine floor that would separate us when we were together again beneath the ground of a city in which even the flowers prey on the weak. I turned around. I nodded good-bye to the priest and workers. One of them, a slim black man with snake-like eyes, told me not to linger. So far that week there had been three armed robberies at burials. And you don't want a nasty scare, he said, looking at my legs. I didn't know whether to take that as a warning or a threat.

I got into the Ford Zephyr and turned around in my seat again and again. I couldn't leave her there. I couldn't leave when I knew how quickly a thief could dig up her grave to steal her glasses, or her shoes, or even her bones, a common occurrence now that witchcraft was the national religion. A toothless country that slits chicken's throats. For the first time in months, I cried with my whole body. I shook out of fear and pain. I cried for her. For me. For the single entity we had been. For that lawless place where, when night fell, Adelaida Falcón, my mother, would be at the mercy of the living. I cried thinking about her body, buried in a land that would never be at peace. When I got in next to the driver, I didn't want to die, but only because I was already dead.

The plot was a long way from the cemetery gates. To get back to the main road, we took a shortcut that was hardly better than a goat track. Curves. Boulders. Overgrown paths. Embankments with no guardrails. The Ford Zephyr went down the same road we'd come up. The driver swerved around every bend. Disconnected, shutdown, I didn't care what happened. We would either die or we wouldn't. Finally, the driver slowed and leaned over the greasy, blackened steering wheel. "What the hell is that?" His jaw dropped. The obstacle spread out before us like a landslide: a caravan of motorbikes.

There were twenty or thirty of them parked across the road, cutting off our route. All were wearing the red shirts distributed by the government in the current administration's first years of office. It was the uniform of the Fatherland's Motorized Fleet, an infantry the Revolution used to quell protests against the commander-president—the name the leader of the Revolution was known by after his fourth electoral victory—and in time that infantry outgrew its role. Anyone who fell into their hands became a victim. Of what depended on the day and the patrol.

When the money to fund the fleet dried up, the state decided to compensate members with a little bonus. While they would receive a full revolutionary salary no longer, they would have a license to sack and raze with abandon. Nobody could touch them. Nobody could control them. Anyone with a death wish and an urge to kill could join their ranks, though in truth many acted in their name without any connection to the original organization. They ended up forming small cooperatives, collecting tolls in different parts of the city. They erected tents and spent the day nearby, lounging on their bikes, from that vantage spying their prey before kicking the bikes into life and hunting them down at gunpoint.

The driver and I didn't look at each other. The band hadn't detected our presence. They were congregated around an improvised altar made from two bikes, on which they'd placed a closed casket. They'd formed a circle around the casket and were laying bunches of flowers and spitting mouthfuls of alcohol on it. They raised their bottles, drank, and spat. "It's a thug's burial," said the driver. "If you're one for praying, then pray, my girl," and he jerked the gear lever beside the steering wheel into reverse.

The time it took him to back up was enough to catch sight of what appeared to be the funeral's liveliest moment.

A ratty-haired woman dressed in sandals, shorts, and a red T-shirt had lifted a girl onto the casket, which she was now straddling. It must have been the woman's daughter, judging by the proud gesture the woman made as she raised the girl's skirt and spanked her backside while the little thing moved in time to the music. With each slap, the girl—twelve years of age at most—shook harder, always to the rhythm of the raucous music that was pumping through the speakers of three cars and the minibus parked on the other side of the curve. "*Tumba-la-casa-mami, pero que-tumba-la-casa-mami, tumba-la-casa-mami,* you-need-to-bring-down-the-house-*mami*," the reggaeton number boomed, charging the air. A grave never had such a steamy lure.

The girl gyrated her pelvis, no expression on her face, indifferent to the teasing and obscenities, indifferent even to the slaps of a mother who looked to be auctioning her young virgin off to the highest bidder. Each time the girl thrust, the men and women salivated and spat aguardiente and applauded. The Ford Zephyr was now far from the scene, but I could still make out a second girl, a little chubby, getting onto the casket and straddling it too, rubbing her sex against the brass plate that was burning with the heat of the sun, beneath which some man was lying stiffly, awaiting putrefaction.

In the heat and steam of that city, separated from the sea by a mountain, every cell of the dead body would start to swell. The flesh and organs would ferment. Gases and acids would bubble. Pustules would attract flesh feeders of the kind that grow in lifeless bodies and scurry around in shit.

I looked at the girl rubbing herself against something dead, something about to become a breeding ground for worms. Offering sex as the final tribute to a life ripped apart by bullets. An invitation to reproduce, to give birth and bring more of his offspring into the world: swarms of people who just like flies and larvae would have brief lifetimes. Beings that would survive and proliferate thanks to the death of others. I would feed those same flies. Each of us belongs to the place where our dead are buried.

The midafternoon radiant heat meant that the mirage that obliterates landscapes had risen over the asphalt, making the concentration of men and women shimmer like a life-and-death grill. We drew farther away and started down a shortcut that was even worse. I could only think about the moment when the sun would drop below the horizon and light would be gone from the hill where I'd left my mother all alone. Then I died once more. I was never able to rise again from all the deaths that accumulated in my life story that afternoon. That day I became my only family. The final part of a life that nobody in that place would hesitate to cut short, machete blow by machete blow. By blood and fire, like everything that happens in this city.

I THOUGHT THREE BOXES would be enough to pack away my mother's things. I was wrong. I needed more. At the dresser, I inspected what was left of the La Cartuja plates. A collection of loose pieces, enough to dish up soup, mains, and dessert for three in a modest household. It was chinaware trimmed with burgundy edging that had a rural scene in the middle. Not much, sincere and modest. I never knew where it had come from or why it was in our home.

In the story of us there was no wedding with a registry, no grandmothers with Canarian accents and Andalusian looks who plied us with fried torrijas that they dished up on those plates during Semana Santa. On that chinaware we placed our steamed vegetables and the sad pieces of chicken that my mother skinned in silence. Eating off them, we honored no one. We came from nobody and belonged to nothing. My mother told me, in her final days, that my grandmother Consuelo had gifted her the eighteen-piece set the day she finally saved enough money to buy the small apartment we'd been renting. A dowry fit for the gardenless kingdom that we founded together.

The chinaware had been left to my grandmother Consuelo by her sister Berta, a woman with Amerindian eyes and black skin who had been married to Francisco Rodríguez. He had asked for her hand in marriage six months after arriving in Venezuela from Extremadura and had built the Falcón guesthouse brick by brick in the heat of the Aragua coast. When he died, everyone started calling Great-Aunt Berta the *musiú*'s widow, a moniker for all Europeans who arrived in the forties, a translation, if it can be called that, of *monsieur*. My mother told me there was only one photograph of the man from Extremadura. It was from the day of his wedding to Berta Falcón, who from that moment forward went by the name of Berta Rodríguez. He, a great hulk of a man, appeared dressed in his Sunday best alongside the striking mixed-race woman, or at least that's what my mother told me about the photo she saw but I never did.

My mother and I ate off the plates of dead people. How many meals must Great-Aunt Berta have cooked and served up on them, day after day? Would she have cooked the repertoire of a woman who moved her large berth around a kitchen smelling of cloves and cinnamon? Whatever the case, those plates emanated just one truth: my mother and I resembled one another only. Through my veins ran blood that would never help me escape. In a country where everyone was made from someone else, we had no one. The land we came from was our only life story.

Before wrapping it in newspaper, I looked at the sugar bowl, never used, that had been forgotten at the back of the dresser. We never sweetened anything we lifted to our mouths. We were skinny like the tree that presided over the dirt patio of the Falcón guesthouse and dropped a dark and sour fruit. We called them "stone plums" because of the tiny amount of flesh and the huge pit. Their centers distinguished them from other fruit. It was almost a pebble, a rough pit rounded off by the sour flesh that gave the small, withered trees, which once a year brought forth the miracle of their fruit, their name.

The stone plums grew in poor soil all along the coast. Children climbed in their branches and stayed up there like crows. Creatures that sipped up the little that the earth gave them. If our trips to Ocumare coincided with the season, we brought back two or three bags chock-full. It was up to me to collect the best ones. My aunts prepared a viscous sweet with them. They let them soak all night and then boiled them with grated sugarcane blocks. After letting the mixture simmer over low heat for several hours, a dark treacle formed. Not just any plum would do, only those that were about to fall from the tree. If they were green, it was better not to touch them; the ones that were still ripening were no good either because they made the treacle bitter. They had to be fully ripe, almost purple, and round and soft.

Collecting them was a painstaking process, accompanied by more than a few instructions.

"Squeeze them like this. Look."

"If it's soft like this, put it in the bag; as for the others, put them aside and wrap them in newspaper later."

"That's so they ripen. If you're not going to explain properly, Amelia, how do you expect her to understand? Don't eat too many. They'll upset your stomach."

"Take this bag."

"Not *that* bag, Amelia. *This* one!"

Clara and Amelia kept interrupting each other. I nodded, then they let me go in peace. I wandered down the corridor and out to the patio. I climbed the tree and started pulling the fruit from the branches. Some came away easily while others resisted, coming free only when I yanked them. When I was done, I gave my aunts the ripest fruit, perfect for the sweet that they prepared in their huge stockpots laden with fruit and syrup. I still remember their silhouettes through the steam, a cloud that always gave me enormous cravings as it enveloped those robust women who tipped kilos of sugar into boiling water and stirred it hard with their wooden spoons.

"Get out of here, girlie. If one of these stockpots falls on your head—" said one.

"You'll be crying all the way from here to kingdom come," finished the other.

I made the most of the scolding to slip away and rescue the small pile of plums hidden in the garden, all for me.

Sitting on the highest branch, I sucked the flesh from them. I sucked and nibbled them right down to the pit, where there was always a little flesh still attached. Eating a stone plum was an act of perseverance. You had to remove the hard skin, then tear and wrench at the flesh with your teeth until you were scraping at the stony heart. Once it was smooth, I swished the pit from one side of my mouth to the other, as if it were a hard-boiled candy. And even though my mother threatened me by saying that if I swallowed the pit a plum tree would grow in my stomach, I enjoyed the smooth feel of it in my mouth. Only when the pits were completely flesh-less did I spit them out, letting fly a slobbery stone that fell to the ground short of my aim, not even grazing the skinny dogs that watched my every move, expecting me to share my afternoon snack. I tried to shoo them away, waving my hands in the air. But they, with their mangy poodle eyes, stayed put, still as statues, watching me eat.

The stone plum tree appeared in my dreams too. At times it sprouted from the city gutters; at others, from our apart-ment sink, or from the Falcón guesthouse laundry. I never wanted to wake from those dreams. Far more beautiful than their real-life counterparts, my dream trees were always full of pearly plums that transformed into glittery cocoons, sleep-ing caterpillars, which I thought were beautiful in a strange and slightly repugnant way. They moved imperceptibly, like the muscles on the horses that sometimes made their way down the road, beasts whose hooves must have been sore from hauling the sugarcane and cacao to the Ocumare mar-ket for the men to unload. That was how everything in the town happened: as if the nineteenth century had never given way to progress. If it weren't for the public lighting and the Polar beer trucks that climbed the road, nobody would have believed that this was the eighties.

So as not to forget those impossible trees that sprouted in my dreams, I drew them in my Caribe sketch pad with wax crayons, choosing the pink and violet colors I found in my box of twenty-four. I used the sharpener to make resin shavings and rubbed those shavings against the paper with my fingertips, giving my grubs a halo effect. I could spend hours on each drawing. I created them with almost as much devotion as when I nibbled and sucked at the sour and veiny plums that to this day are fixed in my memory.

That tree at the Falcón guesthouse was my territory. I felt free on its lonely branch, after climbing it like a monkey. That part of my childhood had nothing in common with the fearful city where I grew up and that, as the years went on, became a jumble of fences and locks. I liked Caracas, but I preferred the sugarcane-and-mosquito days of Ocumare to the city's dirty pavement, which was always strewn with rotten oranges and stained with engine oil. In Ocumare, everything was different.

The sea redeemed and remedied, swallowed bodies and spat them out. It intermingled with everything that crossed its path, like the Ocumare River, which to this day flows into the ocean, pushing at the salt with its fresh water. On the shore grew the sea grape trees with their scant berries that my mother would use to make beauty-queen tiaras for me, while I daydreamed, hidden, my earrings made of pearly caterpillars, of the metamorphosis the plums underwent when they crossed the membrane of reality.

I HEARD GUNSHOTS. Like I had the day before, and the one before that, and the one before that. A gush of dirty water and lead that separated my mother's burial from the days that followed. At my desk by the window in my bedroom, I noticed that the apartments in the neighboring buildings were dark. It wasn't unusual for the electricity to go out across the city, but there was electricity at my place yet not elsewhere, and that was strange. *Something's happening*, I thought. I switched off the lamp. Sharp blows started up at Ramona and Carmelo's place, one floor above. Furniture colliding. Chairs and tables being dragged from one spot to another. I picked up the phone and dialed. Nobody answered. Outside, the night and the confusion worked their own curfew. Venezuela was living through dark days, probably the worst since the Federal War.

A robbery, I thought, but how could that be when nobody had raised their voice? I peered out of the living-room window. A Dumpster was ablaze in the middle of the avenue. The wind was carrying off the cash that neighbors had resorted to burning, huddled in groups. Lean, sooty people who came together to illuminate the city with their poverty.

I was about to phone Ramona again when down below I saw men in military intelligence uniforms exiting my building. There were five of them, and long guns were slung across their shoulders. One had a microwave in his hands, and another had a desktop computer case. Others were dragging a couple of suitcases. I didn't know if I was witnessing a raid, a robbery, or both things at once. The men got into a black van and drove off in the direction of Esquina La Pelota. When they had disappeared into the intersection that led to the highway, a light came on in the neighboring building. Another followed. And another. Then one more. The colossal wall of blindness and silence began to awaken, while a whirlwind of flaming cash spiraled in gusts, propelled by the military truck as it sped off.

Before cash disappeared altogether, the revolutionary cabinet announced, on the commander-president's orders, that paper money would be progressively eliminated. The decree's purpose was to fight the financing of terrorism, or what the leaders deemed as such, but printing more money to replace the old was impossible. The money that circulated forcibly wasn't worth anything, even before it was burned. A napkin was more valuable than a hundred-bolívar bill, which now went up in flames on the pavement like some kind of premonition.

At home there was enough food to last me two months, thanks to a stockpile that my mother and I had made a habit of adding to ever since the first lootings blighted the country years before. No longer out of the ordinary, lootings had become routine events. I was ready to resist thanks to the life lessons they'd given us, which I learned to administer instinctively. Nobody needed to show me how; instead, time was my teacher. War was our destiny, and it had been a long time before we knew it was coming. My mother was the first to intuit it. She made provisions and obtained supplies for years. If we could buy one can of tuna, then we would take two home. Just in case. We stocked the pantry as if fattening an animal that we would feed on forever.

The first looting I remember happened the day I turned ten. We were already living in the city's west. We were isolated from the more violent part. Anything could happen. Filled with uncertainty, my mother and I watched as military platoons passed by on their way to Miraflores Palace, the seat of government, a few blocks from our building. A few hours later, on TV we saw swarms of men and women raiding stores. They looked like ants. Furious insects. Some were heaving legs of beef onto their shoulders. They ran with no thought for the splotches of still-fresh blood on their clothes. Others carried off televisions and appliances they'd pulled through windows smashed with stones. I even saw a man dragging a piano down Avenida Sucre.

That day, during a televised live broadcast, the minister of internal affairs called for calm and civility. Everything was under control, he assured us. A few seconds later, there was an awkward silence. An expression of terror crossed his face. He glanced to one side then the other and left the podium he'd been addressing the nation from. His plea for calm remained just that: a medium-long shot of an empty podium.

The country changed in less than a month. We started seeing trucks stacked with caskets, all of them tied down with ropes, and sometimes not even that. Soon, unidentified bodies were being wrapped in plastic bags and tossed into La Peste, the mass grave where the bodies of gunned-down men and women started fetching up by the hundreds. It was the first attempt by the Fathers of the Revolution to take power, and the first instances of "social unrest" that I remember. To celebrate my birthday, my mother heated a little sunflower oil and fried a maize bollo she'd shaped into a heart. It was a show of love in the shape of a kidney, golden at the edges and soft in the middle. My mother stuck a tiny pink candle in it. She sang "Ay qué noche tan preciosa," a long and catchy national version of "Happy Birthday," which unlike the original lasts a full ten minutes. Afterward she cut the heart into four and spread butter on each piece. We chewed in silence with the lights out, sitting on the living-room floor. Before we went to bed, a burst of gunfire added an ellipsis to that piñataless party that we celebrated in the dark.

"Happy birthday, Adelaida."

The next morning, on the first outing of my tenth year, I met my first love. Or whom back then I understood as such. At school, girls fell in love with all kinds of fantasies: rodents turned into knights errant, princes with delicate features who followed the sweet sounds of a mermaid song along the shore, woodcutters who with a single kiss woke blond-haired, full-lipped sleeping beauties. I didn't fall in love with any of those fictions of masculinity. I fell in love with him. With a dead soldier.

I remember he was printed on the first page of *El Nacional*, the newspaper my mother read every morning at the table from the last page to the first. Not a day of her life went by that she didn't buy it. At least while there was still reams of paper to print it on. If there was a newspaper, she would go down to the newsstand to buy it. That morning she brought it back, along with a pack of cigarettes, three ripe bananas, and a bottle of water—everything she could find at the grocery store, which shut its doors whenever rumors of a new band of looters started circulating.

She arrived home disheveled, puffing, the newspaper tucked under an arm. She dropped the paper on the table and ran to phone her sisters. While she tried to convince them that everything was fine, which wasn't the case at all, I grabbed the newspaper and spread it out on the granite floor. The main photograph, which depicted the military repression and national carnage, covered the entire front page. And that was when he appeared before me. A young soldier lying in a pool of blood. I peered closer, examining his face. He seemed perfect, handsome. His head fallen and lolling on the road's shoulder. Poor, slim, almost adolescent. His helmet was askew, which meant that his head, shattered by a bullet from a FAL rifle, was visible. There he was: split open like a fruit. A prince charming, his eyes flooded with blood. A few days later I got my first period. I was already a woman:

beholden to a sleeping beauty who was killing me out of love and grief. My first boyfriend and my last childhood doll, covered in bits of his own brain, which one shot to the forehead had blown apart. Yes, at ten years old, I was a widow. At ten, I was already in love with ghosts.

I took stock of our home library. On some of the books' covers I could see the colored circles that for so many years, bored and with no parks to play in, I made while my mother imparted her lessons on "subjectverbpredicate." Told not to leave my room, I equipped myself with an armful of books. Sometimes I read from their pages, at other times I only played with them. I unscrewed the lids of the tempera paint pots and pressed them against the bound pages at random: an orange ring for *In Cold Blood* to match the butane color of its cover; yellow, the color of little chicks, for *The Autumn of the Patriarch* to bring out the mustard of the design; burgundy in the case of *For Whom the Bell Tolls*. Almost every book bore a circular mark, as if I'd branded each before returning them to their shelves so they could graze quietly and at ease. Why didn't those marks fade with the passing of time when all our transgressions remain? I wondered, *The Green House* in hand.

Next, I opened my mother's wardrobe. I found her size 36 shoes. Arranged in pairs, now they had the air of a platoon of tired soldiers. I inspected the belts that once showed off her slim waist, and the dresses on their coat hangers. None of her things were garish or over the top. My mother was a fakir. A discrete woman who never cried and who, whenever she gave me a hug, created a paradise around me, a second womb scented with nicotine and moisturizer. Adelaida Falcón smoked and took care of her skin in equal measure. In the university residence hall for young ladies, where she spent five years of her life, she learned both to groom herself and to smoke. From then on, she never stopped reading, gently applying face cream to her cheeks, or quietly drawing on her cigarettes. Those were her happiest days, she often said. Every time she voiced those words, a question burned within me: *Had the years she'd lived with me by her side put an end to the good times of her youth?*

I rummaged around in the back of the wardrobe until I found the blouse of hers that was covered in monarch butterflies. Black and gold sequins were sewn all over it. I'd always loved it to bits. Whenever I removed it from the hanger and held it in my hands, the few square meters of the world my mother and I inhabited were suffused with wonder. The blouse was a swanky version of the glittery cocoons I dreamed about. Magical clothing, made of otherworldly color and fabric. I spread it out on the bed, asking myself why my mother bought it when she never slipped it on.

"How can I step out in that at eight in the morning?" she would say if I suggested she wear it to a PTA meeting. No matter how much I begged, she never went to a meeting wearing the blouse.

I studied at a school run by nuns, a stand-in for a more prestigious institution that wouldn't take me because, at the interview, the principal learned that my mother wasn't married and wasn't a widow either. And although she never said anything to me about the incident, I came to understand it as symptomatic of the congenital disease that in those years afflicted the Venezuelan middle class: the defects of nineteenth-century white Venezuelans grafted onto the chaos of a mixed-race society. A country where women birthed and brought up children on their own, thanks to men who didn't even bother pretending that they were stepping out for cigarettes when they decided to leave for good. Acknowledging this, of course, was part of the penance. The stumbling block on the steep ladder of social ascent.

I grew up surrounded by the daughters of immigrants. Girls with dark skin and light eyes. A summation, centuries in the making, of a strange and mestizo country's practices in the bedroom. Beautiful in its derangements. Generous in beauty and in violence, two of the qualities that it had in greatest abundance. The result was a nation built on the cleft of its own contradictions, on the tectonic fault of a landscape always on the brink of tumbling down on its inhabitants' heads.

Though less exclusive, my school likewise levied restraint on a society that was a long way from having it. In time, I understood that place as the breeding ground for a much greater evil, the natural resource of a cosmetic republic. Frivolity was the least egregious of its evils. Nobody wanted to grow old or appear poor. It was important to conceal, to make over. Those were the national pastimes: keeping up appearances. It didn't matter if there was no money, or if the country was falling to pieces: the important thing was to be beautiful, to aspire to a crown, to be the queen of something . . . of Carnaval, of the town, of the country. To be the tallest, the prettiest, the most mindless. Even now, amid the misery that reigns in the city, I can still make out traces of that defect. Our monarchy was always like that: it belonged to the most dashing, to the handsome man or the great beauty. That's what the whole thing that swelled into the cataclysm of vulgarity was about. Back then, we could get away with it. Our oil reserves paid the outstanding accounts. Or so we thought.

I WENT OUT. I needed sanitary napkins. I could live without sugar, coffee, and cooking oil but not without pads. They were even more valuable than toilet paper. I paid a premium to a group of women who controlled the few packets that made it to the supermarket. We called the women *bachaqueras*, and they acted with as much precision as the leafcutter ants they were named after. They went around in groups, were quick on their feet, and swarmed on everything that crossed their path. They were the first to arrive at the supermarkets and knew how to bypass the caps per person on regulated products. They got hold of what we couldn't, so they could sell it to us at an inflated price. If I was prepared to pay three times the going rate, I could get whatever I wanted. And that's what I was doing. I wrapped three wads of hundred-bolívar bills in a plastic bag. In exchange, I received a packet of twenty sanitary napkins. It cost me even to bleed.

I started to ration everything to avoid having to go out and find it. The only thing I needed was silence. I barely opened the windows. The revolutionary forces used tear gas to repress the people who were protesting the rationing decrees, and the fumes impregnated everything, making me vomit until I was pale. I sealed all the windows with duct tape, except the ones in the bathroom and kitchen, which didn't face the street. I did all I could not to let anything make its way in from outside.

I answered only calls from the publishing house staff, who decided to give me a week's grace period for my loss. I'd fallen behind with revising a few galley proofs. It was in my interest to invoice for the job, but I felt incapable of doing the work. I needed money but had no way of receiving it. There was no connection for carrying out transfers. The internet worked in fits and bursts. It was slow and patchy. All the bolívares I'd deposited in a savings account had been spent on my mother's treatment. As for the pay I'd received for my editing work, there wasn't much left, with an additional problem. By order of the Sons of the Revolution, foreign currency had become illegal. Having any amounted to treason.

When I turned on my phone three messages pinged, all from Ana. One to ask how I was, and two of the kind that get sent by default to a phone's entire contact list. The message stated that fifteen days had gone by with no news from Santiago and asked us to sign a petition for his freedom. I didn't respond. I couldn't do anything for her, and she couldn't do anything for me. We were condemned, like the rest of the country, to become strangers to ourselves. It was survivor's guilt, and those who left the country suffered from it too, a mixture of reproach and shame: opting out of suffering was another form of betrayal.

Such was the power of the Sons of the Revolution. They separated us on two sides of a line. Those who have and those who have not. Those who leave and those who stay. Those who can be trusted and those who cannot. Apportioning blame was just one more division that they cleaved through a society already riddled with them. I wasn't having an easy time of it, but if there was one thing I was sure of, it was that my circumstances could be worse. Being free of death's stranglehold condemned me to silence out of decency.

IN THE MIDST of that night's shoot-out, I realized my neighbor's flush hadn't sounded. I hadn't seen Aurora Peralta since my mother went into palliative care. I was surprised to realize I hadn't heard the irritating pull of the chain, which night after night sounded through my bedroom wall, interrupting my dreams with its gurgle of wastewater.

I knew very little about Aurora. Only that she was timid and dowdy, and that everyone called her "the Spanish woman's daughter." Her mother, Julia, was a Galician who ran a small eatery in La Candelaria, the area in Caracas with the largest concentration of bars run by Spanish immigrants. They were frequented by immigrants from Galicia and the Canary Islands, and by the odd Italian.

Almost all the customers were men. They went there to drink bottles of beer, which they sipped unenthusiastically. Even in the hellish heat, they pecked at chickpea-and-spinach stew, lentils with chorizo, or tripe and rice. Casa Peralta was known as the best place in the city to eat mussel-and-white-bean stew. Judging by the number of diners, that was a fair assessment.

Julia, the owner, had been one of the many Spanish women who made a living from the trades they plied before coming to Venezuela: cooking, dressmaking, farming, waitressing, nursing. Yet, most started out working as housekeepers for the local bourgeoisie in the fifties and sixties; others opened small stores and other businesses. They had only one thing to live by: their hands. Spanish printers, booksellers, and some teachers came to the city too and became part of our lives, bringing with them those resounding, lisped *z*'s that cut through the air in any conversation until they made our pronunciation their own.

Aurora Peralta, like her mother, made a living by cooking for others. For quite some time both before and after Julia's death, she ran the family restaurant. Then she sold it to start up a pastry-making business that she ran from home. Renting premises was expensive, and it was risky: anyone could stage a holdup and take everything she had, not to mention shoot the unfortunate person who at that moment had access to the cash register.

Only nine years separated us, but she already seemed like an old lady. She came over a few times with a cake just out of the oven. Like her mother when she was alive, she seemed affable and generous. And one thing in her life resembled my own: she had no father. Or at least that was the conclusion I came to when I noticed that the life she and her mother led looked a lot like ours. They started and ended each day together, as mother and daughter. I'd been surprised when she hadn't come to my mother's wake. I'd told her in person how poorly my mother was when she'd asked after her health. I assumed the shortages of flour, eggs, and sugar had put a strain on her business, that she was going through a tough time, or had returned to Spain, if she still had family there. Then I forgot about her as easily as I forgot about a faulty lightbulb. I was too busy completing a second gestation, nourished only by my mother, whose presence I could still feel around me. I didn't need or want anything else. No one would take care of me, and I wouldn't take care of anyone. If things got worse, I would earn my right to live by walking all over the rights of others. It was them or me. There was no one alive in that country who was generous enough to give me a coup de grâce. No one would blindfold me or put a cigarette in my mouth. No one would pity me when my time came.

M Y MOTHER'S BELONGINGS were, finally, in boxes to one side of the home library. They looked like baggage that time had packed behind our backs. I resisted the urge to give away or donate all of it. I didn't intend to leave a single page, length of fabric, or splinter of wood to this doomed country going up in flames.

The days accumulated like the dead in the headlines. The Sons of the Revolution tightened the screws. They gave us reason to go out in the street, and all the while the state-sponsored bodies and armed cells repressed those who did, acting in groups with their faces covered, cleansing the pavements. No one was completely safe in their homes. Outside, in the jungle, methods to neutralize opponents reached an unprecedented degree of finesse. Across the nation the only thing in working order was the killing and stealing machine, the pillaging apparatus. I watched them grow and become part of the cityscape, just another feature of everyday life: a presence camouflaged in the disorder and chaos, protected and nourished by the Revolution.

Almost all the militias were made up of civilians. They

acted under police protection. They started congregating by the trash heap at Plaza del Comandante, which we were still calling by its original name: Plaza Miranda, a tribute to the only truly liberal figure of our War of Independence, who died, like other good and just men, far from the country he'd given his all. That was where the Sons of the Revolution chose to establish their new command. *Sons?* I thought. *And why not bastards?* "Bastards of the Revolution," I murmured on seeing a troupe of obese women, all dressed in red. They looked like a family. A gynoecium of roly-poly nymphs: fathers and brothers who were really mothers and sisters. Vestals armed with buckets of water and sticks, femininity in all its splendor and at its most bizarre.

The first day, a convoy of ten soldiers—faceless thanks to dark helmets with skull smiles—camped next to them. After a few weeks, more arrived. All the while more members of the Fatherland's Motorized Fleet turned up. It was impossible to identify them. They wore the masks used by riot police. The lower half of the face was covered with the smiling jawbone of a skeleton and, at the height of the eyes, a piece of rubber was bored with holes. Why did they take such pains to hide their identity when the law was in their hands?

In contrast, the women showed their faces, baring their teeth like menacing dogs. They fought more fiercely. They landed punches. Once they'd managed to bring down an opponent, they dragged him along the ground and stripped him of everything. Everyone carried out their labors with immense gusto, though I never managed to understand what salary could be so high that their fury never abated. What did they get in exchange for the full-time job of smashing heads in as if they were melons? Our days were numbered.

THE LAST BOX fell from the highest shelf of the wardrobe, plowing into my forehead. I picked the box off the floor. "Teseo Shoes," I read. My mother liked these boxes. They were stiff boxes, good-quality, like almost everything in the store. It was called Teseo after the owner, an Italian whose face looked like it had been chiseled from an enormous piece of marble. "Ah, *carissima bambina*," he said after pinching my cheeks so much that they flushed like ripe mangoes. His manner of speaking was always the same, a mixture of Italian and Spanish that he never corrected, despite living in Venezuela for more than twenty years.

People called him "Señor Teseo," as if something in his appearance exonerated him from being called by his first name alone. He was tall, with light eyes and a perfect smile, his teeth large and square. At almost fifty years of age he still had a gallant appearance: a strong jaw, a nose that could belong to a statue, and hair slicked back with gel. He always smelled like eau de cologne and wore a wristwatch almost as big as his large hands. I would be lying if I said that I once saw a single crease in his shirt or trousers. His clothing suited the store he owned, which was on the lower floor of a building built in the fifties, one of the granite-and-mosaic marvels that imposed order in a nation eager to shake off its horse-riding *montoneras* past. Development as an attempt to saddle a lawless nation with progress.

His store was directly across from the apartment block where my mother and I lived. It was a simple, elegant store. The floor was covered in beige carpet. Loafers and high heels lined the showcases, glassed-in stands in which socks and metal shoehorns were neatly arranged. The cash register with its paper rolls spitting out receipts stirred a thorough fascination in me. But that wasn't what I most liked about the store. Another object monopolized my attention: a photograph of Pope John Paul II, which presided over the door to the storeroom. The image seemed to have traveled through time, as if it had frozen the moment when the pope clasped the hand of a young man dressed in a dark cassock.

While my mother took her time requesting shoe sizes that were never quite right, and while Teseo went from one side of the store to the other in search of the perfect fit, I studied the portrait. A pope—no, *the* pope. *Holy moly*, I thought. *What relationship could exist, beyond one of faith, between Señor Teseo, the young priest in the black cassock, and the Great Chancellor of the Holy Glory of God on Earth, in my aunts' words—the very man who presided over Sunday Mass on the official channel on TV?* (At that stage the state hadn't yet declared war on the Church, and the Sons of the Revolution weren't a concern.) *The Vatican*, I thought. So far away.

"Are you related to the pope?" I asked.

After letting out a hearty laugh, Teseo told me the story. The young priest John Paul II was greeting was Paolo, his younger brother. The snapshot, blown up and exhibited in a golden frame, was of Paolo's ordination.

The Italian told me this with special solemnity, as if his brother's cassock and the position he held in the Vatican elevated him on the social ladder, an invisible one that stretched between this shoe store, in the middle of a Third World city, and the world that his brother inhabited. That was the reason behind his perfect manners and the anticipation of progress that his store represented, which set him apart from other immigrants.

Like Teseo, men and women had arrived in the city from Santiago, Madrid, the Canary Islands, Barcelona, Seville, Naples, Berlin—people who in their countries had been forgotten and who now lived among us. *Muisiúes*, every one. Teseo had nothing in common with the Funchal bakers, the Madeira gardeners, or the builders from Naples, people whose hands, though they were thick like Teseo's, were cracked and flaking from working directly with the earth, cement, or flour. People who broke rocks, baked loaves of bread, and built a place already partly their own.

Men like Teseo had disembarked in Venezuela at a time when everything was yet to be done, while the birthplace they'd left behind was in ruins. The streets of Caracas echoed with the voices and accents of people who had crossed the Atlantic, the ocean where someone was always waving good-bye. Their words and names merged with the hubbub of *myloveary*—my queen, my love, my life—that we used and they ended up adopting. People who improvised quick fixes for the nation: the one that theirs and ours formed. We were, together, all that we understood as "ours." The sum total of the shores separated by a sea.

"*Adelaida, mi amore,*" Teseo asked me once, in a Spanish of his own invention, "why do you like that photo?"

"Because I like Rome."

"*E perché?*"

"Because it's on the other side of the ocean and I've never crossed the ocean."

Teseo was holding a metal shoehorn, which fell suddenly to the ground.

"On the other side of the ocean . . ." he echoed.

"Señor Teseo, excuse me," said my mother, who had been walking back and forth for a while now, trying out a pair of navy-blue loafers. "I think I need another size. These are tight on my right foot."

"The next size then, Doña Adelaida. Coming right up . . . On the other side of the ocean. *¡Dall'altro lato del mare!*" We heard him repeating the phrase as he disappeared into the storeroom.

He came back five minutes later, a shoe of the same style in hand, but in a larger size. My mother tried the left one first, then the right. She walked back and forth, regarding herself in the mirror. She took off the shoes. She set them aside and turned to me.

"What do you think?" she said, looking me in the eye.

I let out a silly wolf whistle and gave her a thumbs up.

"I'll take them."

The Italian clicked his fingers, let out a "Bravo!," and crossed to the cash register. He punched in the price and pressed a button that popped open the tray of coins and bills, sorted according to color and denomination. My mother extracted two bills from her purse and handed them over. He passed her the change, in green twenty-bolívar bills printed with the face of José Antonio Páez, the unruly Federal War general who taught himself to appreciate Wagner.

"If you find them uncomfortable, you can exchange them whenever you wish, Adelaida."

"Thank you, Teseo. Adelaida, hija, say good-bye."

"Adios, Señor Teseo."

"Adios, little one, and don't you forget . . . Dall'altro lato del mare," he said with a smile. "Repeat after me: Dall'altro lato del mare."

"Dall'altro lato del mare," I said, and he smiled again, flashing those large, square teeth.

My mother and I stepped onto the street holding hands. She with her bag of shoes and I with the feeling that I'd made a misstep somehow.

"Adelaida, hija, what did you say to Teseo?"

"Dall'altro lato del mare."

"But why did he say that to you?"

"Because he lives in two places at once, Mamá. His family lives there and he lives here. Didn't you see the priest in the photo?"

"What about him?"

"It's his brother, he works with the pope." She looked at me, not seeing the logic in my argument. "That's the thing,

Mamá: Señor Teseo has two homes. One here and another on the other side of the ocean. Do you see?"

"Yes, hija, I do."

I was born and raised in a country that took in men and women from other lands. Tailors, bakers, builders, plumbers, shopkeepers, traders. Spaniards, Portuguese, Italians, and a few Germans who traveled to the ends of the earth to invent ice all over again. But the city started to empty. The children of those immigrants, people who bore little resemblance to their surnames, started heading back across the ocean to countries that were home to other people, searching for the stock with which their own country was built. Unlike them, I had none of that.

I opened the box printed with the Teseo business logo. Inside shone a pair of heels yet to be worn.

A MAN WITH GUNSHOT wounds on a sheetless bed whooshed in front of me, the bed pushed by two nurses at top speed.

"Come on, come on, come on, he won't make it!" they shouted. A ferrous smell invaded my nostrils. It wasn't an odor, it was a warning.

I moved through the Sagrario Clinic corridors, wanting to fire words at someone. Clara Baltasar hadn't shown up for work at City Hall for the past three weeks. So said the guards when I asked after her. Three women surprised her a couple of blocks from City Hall, dragged her inside a Jeep with tinted windows, and kicked and struck her. They left her out the front of her house, as if, instead of a blood-soaked mess, she were a message. "Next time, she won't come back alive." That was what the message meant. Compassion as another form of cruelty. Stopping short of killing her only to prolong her agony.

"An ordinary crime. But nobody saw anything, nobody heard anything," said a City Hall security guard, a man with a small, well-defined mustache and tiny lips that he was pursing like an anus, a show of false discretion that everyone was wearing. The cobbled seam of shame and fear.

Finding Clara Baltasar's room wasn't easy. A nurse who didn't appear to have slept in weeks, a bundle of blackened pages in hand, greeted me.

"Who are you looking for?"

"Clara Baltasar."

"Hmm . . ." she shuffled through the papers for a few minutes. "She's in intensive care. Are you a family member?"

"No."

"Then you can't go up."

"But what about her. How is she?"

"I can't give you that information."

"Is she . . . in a bad way?"

"She's alive," she said before disappearing down the corridor with its filthy tiles.

Long lines of people had filled the stairs of the Sagrario Clinic. Broken, listless people. Men, women, and children waiting their turn in the anteroom of the hereafter. They all looked skinny, punished by day-to-day hunger, mired in the fury of those who no longer remember having lived any better.

There were three groups: those waiting to be put on a waiting list for outpatient operations; those wanting to book in for major surgery; and the third, made up of people silently waiting to see a doctor or to be taken somewhere other than the corridor, already overflowing with people who'd been camped there for weeks.

The whole place, worse than the clinic where my mother had died, was awash with drool and a sour odor, a flatulent smell of beings in the throes of decay. Every now and then, a nurse with a page-filled folder passed by and read aloud, "Amador Rodríguez; Carmen Pérez; Amor Pernalete . . ." A few people looked up and raised their hands; others got to their feet to demand an explanation as to why those people and not them. The defeated were the worst. Shut down, like broken appliances. One, two, three, four, five days, six, seven, eight, nine, ten. "Take a number." "Come back tomorrow." "Not now, tomorrow." The nurses, dressed in worn-out blue overalls, told people to go back to their spots and wait. To have come such a long way, only to die waiting.

"They promised the process would be quicker," a woman said to her daughter.

Promised. That there would be no more stealing, that everything would be for the people, that everyone would have the house of their dreams, that nothing bad would happen ever again. They never stopped promising. Under the threat of nonfulfillment, unanswered prayers crumbled beneath the weight of the resentment fueling them. The Sons of the Revolution weren't responsible for anything that happened. If the bakery was empty, the baker was to blame. If there were shortages at the pharmacy, even of a simple box of contraceptives, the pharmacist was to blame. If we reached home exhausted and hungry and with only two eggs in our shopping bag, the person who'd bought the egg we needed was at fault. Hunger gave rise to a long list of hates and fears. We found ourselves wishing ill on the innocent and the executioner alike. We were incapable of differentiating between them.

A dangerous energy was going haywire inside us. And with it, the urge to lynch those who repressed us, to spit at the soldier who resold regulated goods on the black market, or the smart-ass who tried to deprive us of a liter of milk in the long lines that snaked outside the doors of every supermarket on Mondays. Terrible misfortunes made us happy: the sudden death of a leader, drowned without explanation in the roughest river of the central plains, or a corrupt district attorney getting blown up when he turned the key in his luxury all-terrain vehicle, setting off a bomb hidden beneath his seat. Our determination to get our share of the spoils was such that we forgot compassion.

Those men and women wore an expression I'd started to recognize on my own face when I looked in the mirror: a vertical furrow between my eyebrows. Soon our days were littered with the detritus of war, not normal life: cotton buds, gases, medications, dirty beds, blunt scalpels, toilet paper. Eat or heal, nothing else. The next person in line was always a potential adversary, someone who had more. Those who were still alive fought tooth and claw for the leftovers. Fighting for a place to die in a city devoid of resolutions.

I went up to the seventh floor. Same as in the clinic where my mother died, the elevators didn't work. Up each flight of steps, I came across people who were dying alongside others with minor injuries, children with cuts on their foreheads and elderly people with hypertension. They were piled together, languishing in their own disgrace.

In the intensive care waiting room were two women. They were my age, but they seemed to have aged prematurely. They were resting on a row of blue plastic chairs. They had blankets, food wrapped in foil, and bags packed with folded sheets. Just as I'd done a few weeks earlier, they had put up their own field hospital in the war without tanks endured by those who had to watch their loved ones die. I walked over to the younger. The other was asleep on her shoulder. I assumed they were sisters.

"Are you Clara Baltasar's daughter?"

"Who are you? What do you want?"

"My name is Adelaida Falcón."

"Mmm . . ."

"Your mother helped me get money together to pay for my own mother's treatment. I went to find her at City Hall. They told me she was here."

"I don't know what you're talking about."

"I just wanted to say thank you."

"Get out of here." She got to her feet, waking the other.

"What's going on, Leda? Who is this?" She rubbed the sleep from her eyes.

"My name is Adelaida Falcón. Your mother, Clara Baltasar, helped me get money together to pay for my mother's treatment," I repeated.

"Leave, please. We don't know her. We don't know who you're talking about."

"I just came to tell Clara that my mother died. And I brought her this." I held out two boxes of antibiotics.

They looked at each other, not saying a word. I left the antibiotics on the only empty chair, then turned and left.

Clara Baltasar—the social worker who lined up for people who couldn't go to the supermarket on the designated days—was dead, or was about to die, thanks to a beating the revolutionary commanders had inflicted to make an example of her. I left her the last boxes of my mother's medication.

I went down the seven floors on foot. A woman started weeping loudly upon arriving in the ER. Her father was the man with the gunshot wound that two nurses had pushed past me earlier. He had died before reaching the operating room. They cut us down like trees. They killed us like dogs.

IT WAS MY FIFTH VISIT in three days, but the baker acted as if he'd never seen me before. The flour hadn't arrived this week either. Next to me, two women hauled bags that far exceeded the daily ration of bread that we lined up for only to go home with our hands empty. They left with loaves of bread meant for other people, who missed out no matter how long they waited or how early they rose.

I went up Avenida Baralt, thinking about the white frogs that stuck like stones to the mosquito nets in the Falcón guesthouse. Creatures ensconced in the back of my mind, a bad memory that now bubbled to the fore. We were alike, the frogs and I. Ugly-skinned females that spawn in the middle of tempests.

I reached my apartment door dragging my feet. I turned the key, but the lock stuck. I pushed and pulled. I rattled the peephole grille, pressed on the handle, persisted. There were scrapes around the lock. Someone had changed it. What next sprang to mind were the sleeping mats, the nights camping out, the motorbikes, the caskets, the bruises, the beatings with buckets of water and sticks. A barb of fear pierced me as it dawned that I was too late. My home! Their whole purpose had been to invade every apartment in our building. The troupe of women who had been camped in Plaza Miranda for days was in fact an invasion command. "Dammit!" I put my hand on my crotch. It was damp. I tried to contain the drops of urine and stay calm.

I crouched, looking for shadows that might signal steps. Nothing. I was incapable of perceiving anything other than a faint haze of light. With my hands still between my legs, I quickly went down to the building entry and kept watch. Soon some women appeared. There were five of them and they were loaded with bags, mop handles, and packets of food sealed with a logo I recognized as the Food Ministry's. The ministry was a recent invention; through it, the Sons of the Revolution distributed food in exchange for political support.

The women got into the building using one of the keys from the bunch they were carrying. They were all wearing the civil militia uniform of red shirts. They seemed to have found a pack with the smallest sizes. The tight jeans emphasized their thick legs, below which elephantine feet were shod in plastic flip-flops. They had dark skin and bristly, stiff hair gathered up in untidy mops.

I retreated to spy on them from behind a brazilwood and a few dry ferns shriveled in a corner of the mezzanine. There wasn't much point, but I had to hide behind something. My face was hot, and my underwear was cold. Urine was still escaping as my desperation increased. Fear made me ashamed, dismantling me.

The women had no leader, or at least no obvious one. They took almost an hour to shift their pillows and boxes to the building entrance. Many of them sprawled across the boxes of food, sometimes using them as stools, sometimes as beds. They didn't seem to be in much of a hurry, and were even giving the impression that they were killing time. Some of them looked at their smartphones, raucous music emanating from them, while others chatted among themselves and aired their complaints.

"Roiner the Barinas guy went to San Cristóbal, you know."

"What's with that?"

"What do you think, stupid? Get a higher price for fuel there. You can score a slab of beer with two drums. And the hustle is better, he said. Less competition."

"Sonofabitch, what about us?"

"I'll smash your face in for cussing if you're not careful."

"And what did they give the stinker in Negro Primero?"

"That front's over."

"How come?"

"Oh, world, what am I to know?"

"Look, Who-endy."

"Wendy, it's Wendy . . . not Who-endy."

"That then. . . . You're not gonna call La Mariscala?"

"Hold up, chica. She'll be the one to decide when we move all this."

"And what the hell are we to do until then?"

"What we always do, hang tight."

Around them, mountains of boxes, sticks, mattresses, and almost twenty government-logo-stamped boxes of food. The people who were given those packets had certain obligations: to show up without question at any event or demonstration in support of the Revolution; and to deliver simple services that went from denouncing neighbors to forming commands or groups in support of the Revolution. What began as a privilege for civil servants spread as a form of propaganda and then of surveillance. Everyone who collaborated was guaranteed a box of food. It wasn't much: a liter of palm oil, a packet of pasta, another packet of coffee. Sometimes, if you were lucky, they gave out sardines or Spam. But it was food, and hunger had a tight hold on us.

The women, who were of cathedral proportions, stayed put until a phone rang, and after answering and letting out a few monosyllables, Wendy took to her heels.

"Pick up all this shit right now!"

They picked up the boxes without making too much noise. They made their way two by two, the boxes in hand. There was no electricity in the building, so they had to walk up the stairs instead of taking the elevator. I hid in one of the garbage rooms and waited for them to go up at least one or two floors. From below I couldn't see much, but after a while I guessed they would have reached the third floor. I went back down to the lower floor to make sure they didn't leave anything behind that they'd need to come back for. They'd collected everything. I followed them, dazed by the vinegary smell wafting in their wake. Those women sweated like truckers. Their smell was dark and bitter. A mixture of citrus, onion, and ash. When they reached the fifth floor, my own, I prayed they would keep going. I crept as close as I dared to the balustrade and confirmed what I'd dreaded. They were outside my apartment. My hopes melted in a flash when I heard them shouting for someone to open up and let them in.

They took another ten minutes to move the boxes from the corridor into the apartment. They were tired. They'd carried all that weight up five floors without pause. I'd barely had time to think what I should do. Thirst was burning my tongue, and my bladder was about to burst. When they finished unloading everything and closed the apartment door, I squeezed my eyes shut. I gathered the little courage still coursing through my body and went up the stairs.

I pressed the doorbell. Once, twice, three times.

They took their time answering.

I tried once more, this time rapping my knuckles against the timber.

Then the door opened. A woman, her tangle of unkempt hair pulled up into a bun. She was wearing flip-flops and had tatty polished nails and thick toes eaten up by chilblains.

She was wearing my mother's sequined butterfly blouse.

"What do you want?" she asked, looking me straight in the eye.

"I . . . I . . ."

"I what, girl? What's wrong?"

"I . . . am."

"Uh-huh. You are . . ."

"I . . . am."

I couldn't finish my sentence. I fainted.

W HAT DID YOU DO TODAY?"
    "I helped clean the *pileta*."
"The pool, Adelaida, the pool."

A puddle of green water surrounded by cement in a Caracas preschool. That was a pileta, to my mind, an exceptional thing, a made-up noun. I even came to think that it was the only pileta in the world, and that the word was created especially for that pond, the centerpiece of the patio where we preschoolers played. Sometimes it filled with larvae that were minuscule, springy, fluorescent. I would spend my half-hour recess watching them writhe in the still water.

"Adelaida, come here. Enough with the pileta!"

Verónica, my teacher, was Chilean, and had come to Caracas from Santiago with her husband and two children. Pinochet's dictatorship was the reason behind their decision to leave, she explained to us once as she made sure we drank all our morning tea.

"Who is Pinochet?" I asked, a mayonnaise sandwich in hand.

"A president."

I found that explanation absurd. What did the president of a country have to do with the fact that individuals, out of nowhere, packed their things and left forever?

Verónica must have been my mother's age. Her fair, sensitive skin made her face look like paper. Her hair was cut short, and very dark. A sadness was buried deep inside her and sometimes showed on her face, betraying her at the most unexpected moments: while we organized the toothbrushes of the children who would arrive for the afternoon session, while she sang faded songs about women who would drown in the ocean, and especially when a father or mother would ask how "things" were in Chile.

"You know how it is, back there everything's going from bad to worse," she would respond.

The person who most stopped to talk with her was Alicia's mother. Alicia looked like the cartoon character Heidi and never said much. Anytime someone mocked her accent, which fell somewhere between Argentine and Venezuelan, she would grab the offender by the arm and sink her teeth in. After each episode, her mother came to see Verónica, who had called her in to discuss Alicia's behavior.

They chatted for twenty or thirty minutes and then went out to the recess patio, which Alicia's mother crossed with an elegant gait enhanced by the wonderful, unique clothing she always wore, tights covered by a long, breezy skirt that she lifted to show us her shoes. Her black hair shone, and she always wore it in a bun.

She was a classical ballet dancer, but earned her living dancing for Ballet de Marjorie Flores, a folkloric ensemble that enlivened the interludes of *Sábado Sensacional*, a variety show that played on weekend afternoons. The program featured anyone from children with a talent for singing to international stars on tour that week, and it finished at eight, right before dinner. She always appeared in the dance troupe. She would do a flashy solo, tap dancing a *joropo*, making her floral dress shiver, or else she danced a tango she'd learned when she was in Argentina. At least, so said Alicia one day. Her father, an Argentine editor and journalist, met her mother on one of the tours she did around the southern cone. They married soon after and settled in Buenos Aires. But I only wanted to hear about her mother's skirts.

"Look, Mamá! It's her, it's her!"

"Who, Adelaida?"

"Alicia's mother, the one I told you about, the one from Ballet de Marjorie Flores!"

"What a cheesy name for a dance troupe, my goodness!"

"Hurry, come see!"

"Hold on, let me find my glasses."

Then the two of us waited, planted before the TV, until she appeared: dark, as Venezuelan as could be, with her big white smile and Llanera del Arauca skirts.

"Yes, she's beautiful," my mother conceded, and one day bought tickets to see her dance at the city theater.

My mother couldn't pick out Alicia's mother among the huge corps de ballet of white swans that glided from one side of the stage to the other, enveloped in fog. She maintained that she wasn't there. I thought I recognized her among four dancers who did a pas de quatre to the sounds of an oboe.

The following Monday, after class, my mother overcame her shyness and introduced herself. We went over to her, holding hands, to tell her we'd been to see *Swan Lake*.

"You're from Ocumare—I'm from Maracay, so close!" said the ballerina.

"They're right next door."

"Right by each other! I haven't been to Maracay since I got back from Argentina."

"Oh, my, Argentina?"

"My husband is from Buenos Aires, you see, but we had to leave—"

Verónica had come over to join us. Beneath the midday sun, Alicia with her mother and I with mine, we witnessed how Verónica's face dropped.

"You had to leave Chile too, didn't you?" said Alicia's mother.

"That's right, I had to get away from there."

In that preschool we called pools *piletas*, and Verónica said "there" instead of Chile or Santiago, as if choosing that word emphasized how far away it was. "There" was the past. A place they'd departed with the condition that they never mention it again. A word that smarted like the stump of an amputated arm.

I WOKE OUTSIDE the apartment door. My head was hurting. I couldn't hear a thing. No footsteps or voices. It was as if the twenty families who lived in the building had vanished. My handbag was lying open at my feet. Someone had stolen the little I had in it, my keys and phone. My IDs were still in my purse. My money, not a chance. I realized there was a metallic taste in my mouth. A familiar, raucous tune was coming from the apartment. "Tumba-la-casa-mami, tumba-la-casa-mami, you-need-to-bring-down-the-house-mami." It was the reggaeton number from the cemetery, now booming from inside my apartment as if this were a block party.

I struggled to my feet and staggered around the dim corridor. The smell of sweat and garbage hovered in the air. I rapped at the door. The music was so loud that even I couldn't perceive the thudding of my knuckles against the wood. I banged on it again; nothing. Laughter reached me from the other side, as well as the clinking and clanging of glasses and cutlery. I banged even harder. The same woman as before opened up. She was still wearing the monarch butterfly blouse, which strained at her belly. Everything about her was

73

over the top: her physique, her stink of sweat and cheap perfume. Every muscle and gesture gave off head-honcho vibes that were almost obscene. This was La Mariscala, then. The pinnacle of the miserable, violent army currently laying the city to waste.

"You again, chica? So you're over your fainting spell?"

She looked me up and down. She was clutching a mop handle.

"I . . ."

"Yes, right. . . . You, what?"

"I'm the owner of this apartment. This is my home. Get out of here or I'll call the police."

"Let's see, my love, did hitting your head make you stupid or were you born that way? We're the authority around here. The au-tho-ri-ty."

All I could see was the gap where one of her canines should have been.

"Get out of here," I repeated.

"The only one leaving here's you."

I ignored her and tried to peer inside. La Mariscala grabbed me by the arm.

"Hey hey hey! You be careful now, you know what could happen to you if you get worked up."

"I want my books, I want my plates, I want my things."

She looked at me with calf-like eyes devoid of all intelligence. Without easing the pressure she was exerting on my arm, she lifted her blouse, a few sequins falling from it. A revolver was pressed against her gut, tucked into leggings that were smothering her circumference, making her resemble raw sausage filling overflowing its casing.

"Do you see this pistol, my love?" she said, motioning with her lips. "If I wanted, I could shove it up your ass and blow you apart with a single shot. Couldn't I now? But today, just for today, I'm not going to. If you leave quietly and don't come back, we won't bother you."

"I want my books, my chinaware, my home. Give them back!"

"You want all this? Then you're about to get them, my queen. Wendy, get over here."

The woman approached, scuffing her flip-flops. Her shorts exposed legs covered in scabs.

"What's up?"

"This little lady says she wants some plates and some books, says they're hers. Go fetch them!"

La Mariscala looked at me, defiant. She placed the mop handle to one side and crossed her arms while she waited for her subordinate to bring me my things. She'd left the pistol in full view, pressed against her stomach. The Wendy character came back with a stack of six plates.

"What do I do with these?"

"Give them to me. Now go get the books. Hurry up, we can't wait all day, this little lady was just leaving. Because after this, you're out of here, mamita."

La Mariscala made as if to hand me the stack of plates, holding on to them with both hands. At a glance I could see that wasn't all of them.

"That's not all of them. Where are the rest?"

"What's that, my love? Are you complaining? Here, take your plates."

She let them fall one by one. Each plate in pieces on the granite floor. Crash. Crash. Crash. Crash. And crash.

"You wanted your plates? There, you have them."

"There's tons of books here, I can't carry them all. Here's what I could grab," said Wendy, appearing again in the doorway, this time with five or six volumes.

"Give them here and go to the kitchen, m'hija. See what else is there for us." La Mariscala paused dramatically before snatching the books from her hands. "Let's see what we have here. *The Autumn of the . . . of the . . . Pa . . . Pa . . . Patri . . .*"

"Patriarch."

"Shush. What do you think, that I don't know how to read?"

"Frankly? Yes."

"Well I can, chica. I'm going to do a little demonstration for you. I'll read you a poem!"

She grabbed the volume by its covers, opened it, and ripped it in half. The binding cracked between her enormous hands. The pages came loose like the leaves of a tree. I watched, weary to my bones. La Mariscala laughed, gloated.

"Look at how I treat your things," she said, stomping on the La Cartuja plate shards. "This is what hunger makes us do, my love. And we're hungry." She separated the word into syllables again, adding emphasis to the phrase the commander used to justify their stealing, his way of winning

76

their votes. "With me in charge, nobody will steal out of hunger ever again," he'd said. "No doubt you've never experienced that. You don't know, girl, what hun-ger is. That's right, my love: hun-ger."

She burst into sarcastic laughter and then started stroking her revolver.

"This apartment is ours now. Like everything else, it was always ours, only you took it from us."

I looked at the plates, the torn-out pages, the chubby fingers with no polish on the nails, the flip-flops, my mother's blouse. I lifted my gaze, which she held, enjoying herself. My mouth still tasted of metal.

I spat at her.

She wiped her face, expressionless, and took hold of her pistol. The last thing I remembered was the sound of the butt as it struck my head.

W E WERE EATING blackened chicken with maize *hallaquitas*. We were using plastic forks and coarse paper napkins, a quick lunch before heading back to Caracas. It was hot, and the cicadas were singing like crazy, rubbing their legs to call down the rain. The air smelled of butane, gasoline, engine oil, and pork rinds.

"You're not going to let go of that egg, even to eat?" my mother huffed. "Putting it on the table so you can eat like you've been taught won't do it any harm. Use the cutlery and the napkin, please."

"If I let go, it might roll off. The chicken inside it will die."

"For that little chicken to hatch it needs the mother hen's heat. Even if you keep holding it in your hands, it won't grow."

"Yes, it will. And I'll have a little yellow chick. You'll see."

I left some of my chicken and nibbled reluctantly at a half-eaten hallaquita. We collected the paper plates and tossed them into a Dumpster overflowing with pork, blood sausage, and fried plantain leftovers that stray dogs were pouncing on, hungry. We walked past stalls selling soft toys covered in grease and dust, as well as lottery tickets and folkloric music tapes. I stopped before a counter piled with local treats. Flies and wasps were wheeling around the homemade candy, coconut bites, guava paste, and sticky scrolls covered in treacle.

"If you eat any of those your teeth will fall out. And who knows what water they use, or the conditions they make them in," my mother said while I salivated at the sight of a caramel bar wrapped in plastic.

"I didn't say I was going to eat it. I'm just looking at it."

"I'll do you a deal. If you let go of the egg and leave it behind, I'll buy you one of those treats. Whichever one you want."

"I'm not leaving it."

"Not even for a candy? Or a coconut bite? Yummm—how can you resist?"

"I want the chick, Mamá."

"When the egg breaks on the way home, you'll be sorry. You'll have sacrificed the treat for nothing."

"I won't have, I want a little chick."

My mother held out a twenty-bolívar bill, a long rectangle of green paper. Back then they were worth their actual denomination: twenty bolívares. Not twenty million, not twenty bolívares fuertes—the ones they added zeros to, then seized to hide how little they were worth. Of the money that existed before the Sons of the Revolution, this was the bill I most liked. Twenty bolívares back then was enough to buy three or four breakfasts. Several kilos of anything. It was a fortune.

"I'll take one coconut bite," my mother said to a toothless

woman who was smoking with the flame *pa' dentro*—their cigarettes back-to-front—as she cooked arepas on a griddle.

The woman took the bill. She passed her right hand over her forehead, placed the bill to one side, and shaped a coconut bite. Then she transferred it to a brown paper bag. She gave my mother her change and passed her hand over her forehead once more. She took the saliva-soaked cigarette from her mouth, exhaled a mouthful of smoke, and placed the cigarette between her lips again. My mother turned around, looked at the ceiling, and bit the bullet.

"If you put down the egg before you get on the bus, I'll let you have some of this."

"I'm not letting it go."

"Adelaida, I'll give you this coconut bite in exchange for your egg. You love these!"

"Not happening."

She put the treat in her bag, grabbed me by the hand, and strode toward the bus that would take us back to Caracas. After waiting our turn to get on, she took out the treat and started making exaggerated, greedy sounds.

"Yum, it looks so good! Smells good too."

I stayed firm. I didn't taste the treat, or let go of the egg I'd found on the floor of the Falcón guesthouse chicken coop. I wanted to see the chick emerge from its shell.

We sat in silence for the entire trip. My mother, worn out, slept with her purse on her lap. I, tyrant queen and occupier of the window seat, examined the small street stalls at the edge of the road: dwarf bananas, mandarins, and cassava cake bathed in treacle; the flowers and crucifixes of make-shift shrines, raised in memory of those who had lost their lives in crashes who knows how long ago. All over the country, the dead menaced on all sides.

Every place is sketched and erased by way of its roads, in the routes that stretch from the periphery to the center. Time and again we journeyed from the sea to the mountains. We travelled the miles separating some people from others. We crossed valleys planted with sugarcane, rosy trumpet trees, and *araguaney* trees in silence.

I was still clutching my small, pale egg. I cupped my hands around it, waiting for the heat of my body and the long trip to deliver a living being.

My mother woke as the bus was pulling into its bay in the metropolitan bus terminal. She seemed to have aged during the trip. She got out of her seat with robotic movements. She asked if I was thirsty, if I needed to go to the bathroom. I said no to everything. She grabbed her bag, checked that we had everything, and gave me a kiss.

We got off the bus dragging our feet, our belongings in tow. We got into an old taxi, a run-down Dodge with broken headlights and dents in the door. Back then we called them *libres*, not taxis. The driver dropped us at our building entrance. My mother unloaded everything on her own: the small suitcase and the bags full of stone plums. She paid with a crumpled bill.

We waited for the elevator. We went up through the rusty throat of our old building in silence. Once inside, my mother called my aunts to let them know we were home safely. I, encumbered as I was with the egg, had forgotten to tie my shoelaces. For a moment—the only time I'd let go of it that day—I placed the egg on the kitchen table. I crouched and started tying my shoes. When I was about to tie the final bow, the egg fell to the granite floor. It smashed next to my left foot. The beige shell shattered into a thousand pieces.

The egg white splattered all over the floor. In the yellow yolk, I saw a little red spot: the small amount of life I'd breathed into the egg with my hands, which had proved themselves incapable of delivering anything. My mother came back into the kitchen and saw the disaster. The egg, my face. She took the coconut bite in its paper bag from her handbag. She looked at it in disgust and threw it into the bin.

"I'm turning on the water heater. When the water warms up, get in the shower. I'll take care of this."

She cleaned up the disaster. I got in the shower. I rubbed a jasmine-scented bar of soap all over my body while the water washed the hours spent in the bus from my skin. The useless wait on that trip home.

S TITCH YOU ALIVE, I do; stitch you alive, I will."
On contact with my skin, the needle smarted and burned. I cried tears of pain.

"Stitch you alive, I do; stitch you alive, I will."

"María, you're hurting me. It's hurting! Leave it be, already. Leave it!"

"Shhh, you should have thought of that. Quiet, let me work. Stitch you alive, I do; stitch you alive, I will."

Before becoming a nurse, María, my sixth-floor neighbor, had dreamed of becoming a seamstress. Her mother had made a living sewing clothes and mending the garments that others brought her. She did wonders with very little, María told me as she passed the surgical thread through the eye of a sterilized needle.

"You know, I always wanted to sew like my mother. She hemmed pants with the same care and attention that she paid wedding dresses. Imagine! Back then, there weren't nearly as many stores as there are now."

"María, please, you're hurting me!"

"Remember the narrow little alleys in La Pastora? Up there . . . do you remember or not?"

"I do, but María, you're hurting me!"

"Well, my mother opened a store in one of them. She attracted a steady stream of customers, especially brides, who would have a fitting the day before the ceremony."

"María, please . . . please! Enough already!"

"Shhh. Calm down, honey. Hush, and listen. My mother would do the final stitches in the hem while her client was still wearing the wedding gown, and she would repeat: 'Stitch you alive, I do; stitch you alive, I will.' You know why?"

"María, stop it."

"Shhh, calm down, and listen to the story, it's a good one. My mother would say that if you sew clothes while someone is wearing them, people die. Small-town superstitions, you know. So whenever I quickly mend something for someone, I always repeat that phrase: 'Stitch you alive, I do; stitch you alive, I will.' And yours counts as a quick mend. Because we're not going to pull off your head to stitch it now, are we?"

"María, you're hurting—"

"Grit your teeth; this one will show you the meaning of hurt." And she dug the surgical needle into my skin for the final time. "Stitch you alive, I do; stitch you alive, I will. That's it, there you have it, all good to go. As good as new!"

If I wanted to live, I had to stay awake, alert. María, who insisted that I stay at her place, telling me that she would call my aunts, that for the love of God would I refrain from going out in the state I was in, passed me a glass of sugar dissolved in water. Despite the shot of glucose to my brain, I had to clutch the door frame as I was leaving.

"Young lady, where are you off to? What are you doing? Stay here."

"I'm fine."

"You're *not* fine. Where are you off to?"

"The police."

"What police? What do you mean, the police, honey? You'll only make things worse. Stay tonight, and tomorrow you can call your aunts and leave. Don't even think about putting up a fight with those people. Go to Ocumare. Far away. Tomorrow more of them will arrive. But if you call the police, they'll come in a flash. Don't you understand that those people are in charge now? Don't you understand it, young lady?"

"María, I'm not sure how I can repay you. I'll find a way."

"You owe me nothing, there's nothing to repay. But hear me this: you're not leaving."

"I have to make this right."

"Stay tonight. Tomorrow you can go wherever you want. Your head's got an almighty split in it. At least wait until the pain's gone. I've got a spare room, go lie down; tomorrow you can do whatever you feel like. Though I've said it before and I'll say it again: nobody will stop them, we'll be the ones who wind up paying the price. Young lady: we've already lost this war. There will be more thugs and criminals where they came from. Soon we'll be living in even more fear than we are now."

"More?"

"Listen to me, Adelaida, there's no end to this. We'll never know the limits of this disaster. Stay."

"María, thank you for all you've done . . . but you can't talk me out of leaving."

"Don't go to the police. Do whatever you want, but don't report the incident."

"Good-bye, María."

I went down the stairs to the fifth floor and planted myself before Aurora Peralta's apartment. I inspected the line of light below the closed door, trying to make out shadows or steps. Once again, I couldn't see anything. I stood before the wooden surface covered in white paint. I inspected the lock: no sign of forced entry. I placed my hand on the handle . . . and a miracle happened. Forcing the door wasn't necessary, it was enough just to apply pressure and push. I went in quickly and closed the door in silence. The living-room window was open. Through it blew a foul wind that tasted of lead and brawls. I glanced around the living room, which was very similar to our own. Then I saw her.

Aurora Peralta was lying on the floor. Her eyes were open, and her lips were purple. I didn't know which was worse, the pain in my head, the horror of seeing her like that, or the fear of giving myself away with an hysterical scream.

"Aurora!" I hissed. "Aurora! It's me, your neighbor!"

I placed a finger on her neck to see if she had a pulse. She was cold and stiff. I felt repulsion and pity at once. A thick snake of vomit rose in my throat. I ran to the kitchen sink, identical to ours, and heaved up a bitter juice. I went back to the living room, my legs weak. I looked at her from a distance. Aurora Peralta had become just another corpse in this city of ghosts.

On the counter I found a bowl of eggs that Aurora Peralta had been beating to white peaks when death took her by surprise. The living room with its bare furniture resembled a still life. The sight made me feel a sympathy for her I'd never felt when she was alive. Standing before Aurora Peralta's lifeless body, I saw how the threads of fate that had brought us to either side of the same wall wove together. Aurora Peralta was a corpse and I, Adelaida Falcón, a survivor. An invisible thread united us. An unforeseen umbilical cord between the living and the dead.

I hurried off to find something to drape over her. I wanted to cover her eyes, which right now were gazing at me from the afterlife. I opened drawers, looking for a sheet, towel, or blanket large enough not to leave any of her limbs exposed. In the master bedroom wardrobe I found a white sheet. As I covered her, I kept my eyes shut so that my gaze wouldn't meet hers. I stood and looked over her shape. Then I looked around. If only the walls could talk. Did they kill her? Did she die? Did she suffer a heart attack? Everything was confusing and happening too fast. One thing was certain: she was dead, and I was alive. Who would ask questions about Aurora Peralta's death? Was anyone waiting for her call? Would a relative miss her, a friend, a lover? Or was she, like me, isolated enough that nobody would notice her absence? On the table were three letters, two open and one sealed, next to an uncharged phone and the bunch of keys she'd failed to lock the door with. She must have pushed the door shut without engaging the deadbolt, the reason I'd been able to enter after only pressing the handle downward. Anyone in their right mind would double-check the deadbolt in a city like this. What impulse had made her drop everything to start beating egg whites?

Had La Mariscala and the others killed her? Did they force their way inside and leave when they saw she was dead? Why did they invade my apartment and not this one? I walked around the apartment once more. But there were no signs of violence, not even the mess that burglars make when searching for money or jewelry. Everything seemed to be in order. Aside from the fact, of course, that a dead woman was lying on the floor. The kitchen light had been on all this time. Horror permeated me, an acute, brackish fear. The prickle when you're overcome by the contrary urges to stay and go. But where could I go? I had no place to live. I discarded the idea of going to the police and clung to the refuge I'd found. Think, think, think. Adelaida Falcón, think.

In what until recently had been my home, footsteps were still sounding, louder than the ones my mother and I used to hear from Aurora Peralta. I could distinguish Wendy's flip-flops, La Mariscala's laughter, the activities of people in the process of conquering a territory. The crushing sound of "Tu-tumba-la-casa-mami, tumba-la-casa-mami; you-need-to-bring-down-the-house-mami." The soundtrack to a nightmare. My landline joined that sound track at daybreak when it started ringing without pause for at least twenty minutes. Who was looking for me, and why?

I had a better view of Plaza Miranda from this side of the building. A new patrol of women had taken the place of the previous ones. They were even more corpulent than La

Mariscala and her clan. María was right. They'd have no trouble taking over the other apartments, occupied or not. Accompanying the nine warrior women in the plaza were a few members of the Fatherland's Motorized Fleet. For the moment, they were occupied. They were fighting a group of young men who had been burning banners dedicated to the Eternal Commander.

In no time a convoy of military police officers appeared, as well as a handful of gunmen. I watched them move about, rowdy and bloodthirsty. I wanted to cry out, to warn the young men that there were too many, but my voice abandoned me. The roving gunmen had already brought down two people, a pair of skinny young men who were now lying on the asphalt. One was convulsing and spitting blood from his mouth, like a bull when the matador botches the final sword thrust.

I returned to the living room and took up the only unopened envelope lying on the table. It was from the Spanish Consulate. I tried to read it by holding it up to the light, to no avail. I went back to the opened letters. One, the electricity bill. The other, which likewise bore a stamp featuring a red-and-white flag, a letter from the Spanish government requesting proof that Julia Peralta, Aurora Peralta's mother, was still living, so she could continue to collect her pension. As far as I knew, she had died at least five years before. I folded the consulate of Spain's letter and request in half and tucked them into my trousers, collected the keys, and locked the door.

Aurora Peralta was dead, but I was still alive.

I'D NEVER WITNESSED A BIRTH. I hadn't conceived a child or delivered one. I hadn't cradled an infant in my arms or dried any tears but my own. Children weren't born in our family. Instead, elderly women died, undone in the deathbed of their authority. They even reigned at the foot of a grave, just like those who die at the foot of a volcano. I never understood motherhood as anything other than what my mother and I had: a relationship to be maintained and managed, an unobtrusive love expressed through our keeping the world we'd built for two in balance. I had no awareness of its transformative powers until the day my mother took me to see a painting by Arturo Michelena, a painter I'd thought only depicted battles, who raised before me irrefutable proof that giving birth to a child enlightens, that it clarifies the murk and establishes a raison d'être for the womb's darkness.

It was his canvas *Young Mother* that made me wonder, for the first time, what it might mean to carry a child. I was twelve and the artwork was more than a century old. Michelena painted it in 1889, during his golden era. He was living in Paris, had been awarded prizes in several salons, and had even received a medal at the same World's Fair that featured the Eiffel Tower. Michelena was an Académie Julian alumnus, a moderate cosmopolitan, someone who was a long way from understanding the Salon des Refusés, but he depicted the light of the Valencian valleys in Venezuela as only those who've been educated beneath the glare of the tropics can. The light that burns everything.

I stood before that canvas as if discovering a domestic truth: mothers embody, at the same time, beauty and havoc. Back then I knew nothing of Madame Bovary or Anna Karenina, I ignored the dissatisfied women who committed suicide in the same way I didn't know about the unhappy women poets who would make me a reader. I hadn't read Miyó Vestrini and her *Órdenes al Corazón*, hadn't heard about the Yolanda Pantin's shattering *Casa o Lobo* or Elisa Lerner's *Carriel para la fiesta*. I had read Teresa de la Parra's *Ifigenia*, but had done so with no understanding of the boredom that drove the young lady from Caracas to write. I was a long way from understanding the grandes dames who would make such a mark on my life and yet, standing before that Michelena canvas, I discovered the woman who was already living inside me. I wasn't brave, but I wanted to be. I wasn't beautiful, but I coveted the smooth skin of the fertile woman depicted in that painting before me.

It was Michelena who made me aware of my curves, who illuminated the havoc of my body through his young mother reclined in the rocking chair, a nymph straight out of *The*

Spinners cradling a child far too big, fair, and healthy for a country afflicted by hunger and war. Looking at the tremor of leaves reflected on her skin, puzzling out the false shadows created by the painter's palette, I studied the woman's fleshy form and the slow decline that comes with childbirth. If learning means rectifying one's ignorance, that morning I was dealt a blow: the strange, tidal pull of beauty that mothers emit, beings of faint perfume, women who shine beneath the morning sun.

My mother and I walked along Los Caobos, the boulevard of a Frenchified park that a Catalonian engineer, Maragall, planned for 1950s Caracas. We were coming from a *Peter and the Wolf* show at Teatro Teresa Carreño's José Félix Ribas concert hall, the largest in Venezuela, located just a few steps from the National Art Gallery. An oasis amid the rest of the country. We stopped at the Francisco Narváez fountain to admire the well-built nymphs, Indian women carved in stone who shared similarities with the María Lionza goddess statue, except that these looked sterner. The fountain they were part of, which the sculptor titled *Venezuela*, was in the middle of a great mirror of water that had candy wrappers and faded potato chip bags floating in it. A soup swirling with leaves and scraps.

"Did you like the National Art Gallery?" my mother asked.

"Uhhh," I answered as I sucked on the straw of a peach juice box she'd passed me from her handbag.

"And what did you like best?"

With her question in mind, I fixed my gaze on the exaggerated breasts of Narváez's Indians, then looked down at my cracked white shoes.

"The mother."

"Which one?"

"Michelena's . . ."

"Why's that? I thought you'd like Soto's *Penetrables*, or Cruz-Diez's sculptures."

"I did. But I liked the mother. The one in the dress in the pergola."

"Ah, no wonder," said my mother, condescending. "Because of the pink gown?"

"No," I stayed silent, basting the words in the little amount of juice that was left. "I like it because it trembles."

"Trembles?"

"Yes." I made another slurp. "It moves. Trembles. It is and it isn't. Do you know what I mean? It exists and doesn't exist . . . it comes and goes. It's not a picture. It's alive."

My mother gazed at the water. The cicadas were rehearsing their dry-season racket and the morning was seeping away like a Sunday remnant. The cool marble promenade, not vandalized back then, made me want to curl up and take a long siesta. My mother rummaged in her handbag and got out a packet of tissues that she passed me so I could wipe my mouth.

"And that's why you like it?"

"Uh-huh . . ." I responded, not elaborating further. "When I was born, is that how we looked?"

"What do you mean?"

"Like in that picture: large, pink. You know, like cupcakes."

"Yes, hija. We looked like that." My mother's face crumpled, and she started brushing off her skirt. She closed her handbag and took my hand.

Inside the profound solitude of a tree- and nymph-filled park, something in that country had begun to prey on us.

I STUDIED THE EXITS that led to the parking lot. I did the same for the closest Dumpsters, and for the access to the quieter streets. I needed to dispose of Aurora Peralta's body without drawing attention. If I wanted to stay in her apartment, I couldn't make a single mistake. I discarded the idea of going to the police. I would be more likely to end up in prison than find someone who would believe my story. I waited until ten in the evening. Bursts of gunfire swept the streets. Bullets, real bullets. The corridors were deserted. People had shut themselves in their homes, afraid. Three hours before, La Mariscala and her troupe had left their stronghold to join the melee on Avenida Urdaneta. The Sons of the Revolution and their armed groups slaughtered a hundred hooded protesters: people who went out to be killed, for hunger and anger are motives enough to die. It was time. I couldn't pass up the opportunity that everyone else's confusion and desperation had afforded me.

Dragging Aurora Peralta to the corridor was far more complicated than expected. Her sixty kilos weighed a ton. I didn't know which was worse: her weight or her stiffness. I pressed the elevator button. I could hear the elevator clanking against the girders. It was rising through the insides of the building more slowly than ever. When I opened the door, I realized the space inside was too small. Lying down, Aurora Peralta's body wouldn't fit. Her limbs were stiff as hooks. I couldn't bend her or change her position. My temples were throbbing, my hands trembling. I'd wrapped a shirt soaked in rubbing alcohol over my nose, and now it was suffocating me; meanwhile, my plastic gloves were parboiling my fingers. Sometimes I had the feeling that I wasn't the one who did all this.

Standing as I was, facing the open elevator, exhausted, and with her body lying at my feet, I racked my brains for a way out. Dragging her step by step down to the lower floor would be the easiest way to get caught. I couldn't stay in the corridor either, waiting beside a dead body. The twelve labors of Hercules seemed like trifles compared with this. I knew just one thing and clung to it: this dead woman was the only thing that could keep me alive. I had to play my cards right if I wanted to stay in her home.

I heaved Aurora Peralta's body back along the corridor to the apartment. Changing the direction of her body to put her legs in a straight line toward the door amplified the feeling that I was going around in circles. This first attempt to get rid of her had taken a whole hour and I was still in the same place I'd started. The sound of gunshots, explosions, and breaking bottles fortified me. I breathed in as deeply as I could. Adelaida Falcón, think. Desperation can beget strokes of genius. I looked up and examined the dark apartment. A sewing-machine table against the balcony presented itself as the most practical option. If men and women were killing themselves in the streets, then how strange could it be for a dead body to fall from a fifth floor? May dead bodies rain down. Just that, no metaphors.

I maneuvered the piece of furniture until it was pressed against the window that opened onto the railing. It took me another half hour to lift Aurora Peralta from the floor. I boosted her body onto a chair, in this way gaining the momentum needed to shift her onto the table. The flat surface acted like a large platter. I rolled her facedown. Her legs were stiff as tongs. Rigor mortis gave her the appearance of a sad acrobat. I pushed her, straining with all my strength, as if, rather than doing away with a dead body, I were giving birth. "A mother came to believe/that her daughter conceived/and gave birth thanks to a tempest," my mother used to sing. And that's what this was: a birth.

When Aurora Peralta's waist passed beyond the window frame, the weight of her body made it tip. I watched her stick legs disappear in the air: a bulk robbed of life and dignity. It wasn't my fault. It's not your fault, Adelaida, I told to myself, crouching on the balcony floor. The sound of the Sons of the Revolution's motorbikes drilled in my ears. Their threats and shouts echoed like pellets. "Kill him, kill him! Kill that dog! Film it! Film it, they're taking him! Kill him!" If I didn't hear Aurora Peralta smash into the pavement, it was thanks to all that noise.

I wanted to peer down but instead stayed hidden, slathered in sweat and awash with shame. The stitches María had used to sew up the wound in my head were still hurting.

Heat was plastered to my face. I felt a tide of puke rising up my throat, and it was dense, congealed. Things had reached a point of no return; any attempt to remedy past actions would compromise the next step. I hadn't killed her. But that didn't mean I hadn't dined at the same trash-covered table.

I only wanted a home. Somewhere to lay my head. A place where I could get my bearings and wash the filth from my body. I wished for the water to have its way. I wanted it to cleanse me and dissolve the dirty scar that had formed, like a second skin, over my body. If I wanted that, I had to hurry. I couldn't leave Aurora Peralta's body at the building entrance. Anyone might recognize her. Twenty meters from the door, I spotted a burning Dumpster. If I could take her there, no trace of her story would remain. Just another dead person in the city. One more among many. Weren't quartered bodies always showing up in suitcases and trash heaps? How many corpses that no one would ever recognize or claim dotted the city? People who died. And the story ended there.

I didn't know if I should keep the alcohol-soaked shirt on my face. I needed it to counter the tear gas. But if I went downstairs with my face covered, my appearance would mark me as having taken a side. The losing side, of course. Most protesters used shirts in the same fashion so they could endure hour upon hour of pepper spray bombardment. It was the uniform of the punished: a magnet for the roving gunmen. I grabbed the shirt at the last minute and rushed out into the street. At the building entrance, a burst of pepper spray seared my throat.

Aurora Peralta had hit the asphalt headfirst. I had trouble recognizing her. The stench of burned tires and pepper gas formed a dense cloud, an ideal cover for moving quickly. I dragged her body toward a drum that was burning beside the blaze. It was farther away than I'd calculated. On the way I picked up a bottle filled with gasoline, a homemade bomb that some unfortunate soul hadn't had the chance to throw. I splashed the fuel over Aurora Peralta. I pulled her by the ankles toward the barricade. Her clothing caught alight as soon as it touched the flames. A San Juan bonfire in April.

A song that people in Ocumare and Choroní sang every year on June 23, the eve of San Juan, came to mind. I would hear the crude lyrics in the distance as I stood in the doorway of the Falcón guesthouse. "*'Til the gunfire sounds, I ain't moving from he'. Ay, garabí,*" the town's Afro-descendants would sing, hitting their drums, as men and women moved their hips amid the sweat and aguardiente vapors. My aunts Clara and Amelia knew the lyrics by heart and sang them without blinking an eye. On the beach, everyone partook in the revelries, drunk, elbow to elbow, nervous as larvae, heaving a swaying wooden saint to the seashore.

A few meters from me, Aurora Peralta was being consumed by fire and bullets. People ran from one side to the other, performing their own strange revelries, a fiesta without rhyme or reason comprised of gunpowder, death, and lunacy. In this country we dance, and we purge the dead. We sweat them out, exorcise them like demons, expel them like shit. They'll only end up in the septic tanks, trash heaps that burn easily, as if we were made of worthless stuff. *"Hasta que no suene el plomo, no me voy de aquí. Ay, garabí."* I left Aurora Peralta burning in solitude and ran.

I was almost at the building entrance when I was bowled over. My cheek struck the ground. I felt my skin scrape against the asphalt. I thought I must have slipped on the oil that gets spread across the pavement to bring down anyone who flees. Then I realized somebody had knocked me down. The weight of his body was pinning my hips, immobilizing me.

"Keep still, chica! You keep still! What are you doing, hey? Where are you going?"

I tried to turn around, but the body on top of me wouldn't let me free myself. Pressed against the ground, I couldn't see his face or guess at which side he belonged to—whether he was protesting the government or was one of its followers. I started writhing, trying to get him off me.

"What are you doing, chica?"

Whoever it was didn't seem willing to hit me, at least not straight off.

"What am I doing? I'm defending, fighting like you are."

I squirmed until I was faceup.

"Fighting? You? Against what? Against who?"

My attacker's face was obscured behind a Sons of the Revolution mask. His eyes peered at me through a black facial covering in the shape of a skull. The stench of burning flesh was spreading through the air. Pinning me with his legs and holding my arms down, my attacker only wanted to keep me immobilized. I redoubled my strength, flailed, kicked, and stretched my torso until I freed an arm. I swiped at him, squirmed. Finally my fingernails hooked around his mask. I ripped it from his face. He didn't object, didn't even struggle. He left me a moment, not moving a muscle. If there's a God for wrongdoers, He was by my side. I recognized the face immediately. It was Ana's brother.

"Santiago! It's you!"

He said nothing.

"Your sister's driving herself crazy looking for you."

"Shhhhhh! Do as I say. Keep hitting me and resisting, okay?" He covered his face with the mask again and got close to my ear. "Where can I take you to get you away from this?"

"The apartment block twenty meters behind you."

Santiago lifted me off the ground, pushing and shoving, grabbing and waving about a tear-gas grenade that had exploded nearby. A few seconds later, no one could see us. As a Motorized Fleet band crossed the avenue at high speed, emptying their gun barrels against the buildings, we ran toward the building entrance.

" 'Bye," he said when we reached it.

Then he turned and started walking away. I dashed over to him and tried to pull him into the building, my arm around his neck. Santiago pushed me away.

"Go inside. If you're set on getting shot you can go right ahead, but I'm not getting myself killed. If they find out I didn't split your head in two, they'll shoot me."

A new burst of gunfire sent us sprawling on the ground.

"Please, listen to me. Your sister's looking for you. You have to call her. And if you don't, I will!"

"If you do that, they'll crush us all. Her, me, even you. So—"

He couldn't finish his sentence. A boy fell at our feet. He was no older than seventeen. He'd been pushed by the force of a tear-gas bomb that ripped apart his chest. Right behind him, one of the riot police appeared with a rifle in hand. Santiago dealt me a punch to the stomach, grabbed me by my hair, and shook me like a doll.

"Get this one to the truck. Get going, drag her, you lazy piece of shit, drag her! Take her to the Bolívar command!" the black-clad man ordered Santiago.

Even though I was doubled over on the ground, winded, my stomach muscles clenched, I saw how he moved away from us to make a beeline for his fallen prey. Squatting, he started searching the boy's pockets. Robbing the dead, instead of laying them to rest.

But, after all, what gave me the right to judge him?

Sons of vice, my aunts would say, singing along to the tune dedicated to San Juan.

"Hasta que no suene el plomo, no me voy de aquí. Ay, garabí!"

I HAD NO IDEA where I was until we got to the building entrance. I could barely fit the key into the lock. Santiago was still wearing his Sons of the Revolution mask, so it was hard for anyone to tell whether we were chasing somebody or fleeing. The threat that the mask signaled made us invisible to some, vulnerable to others. A few months before, clothing associated with the government would have given us a free pass, with no one daring to approach. But things had changed. Now many wouldn't hesitate to ambush a member of the regime and lynch him with anyone else who felt like teaching him a lesson. Santiago, an unarmed executioner, was easy prey for anyone who wanted to expend some of the hate that the commander had bequeathed us. Finally we went inside the apartment. Santiago took off his mask and looked in silence at the furniture and the walls. Seeing him like that, with his face pinched and his eyes wild, stirred in me more pity than fear. He turned on the spot, disoriented. He canvassed the messed-up living room. He stumbled over his words. He hit me to save our hides, he said. He was where he was and doing what he was doing because . . .

Poised before his own ellipses, Santiago started over. He hit me to save our hides. This—he brandished the mask—was a nightmare. In three months. The police. The special forces.

"I told you. Told you to go, to get into the building. Why did you follow me, dammit? Now you're in it up to here too, up to here! Do you hear me?" he said, waving a hand over his crown.

Santiago was wrong. The sewage had risen far above our heads. It had buried us. Him, me, the rest. This was no longer a country. It was a septic tank.

"Lower your voice, will you? After the beating you gave me, I'm the one who should be shouting hysterically."

"But you didn't—"

"Yes, I know, I know, I heard you. If you didn't do it, they'd have cut off your balls. But now I'm asking you to follow my rules: the apartment next door has been invaded by a group of women who would have no qualms about kicking us out by burying a gun in our sides. While you're here, speak as little as possible, and when you do speak, make sure it's on this side of the apartment. Don't turn on any lights and don't open the door or peep out if someone knocks."

"But this . . . ?"

"No, Santiago, this isn't my place. And yes, I've got a lot of explaining to do. But you do too. Your sister thinks you're dead. She's heard nothing from you. She keeps paying for them not to kill you, and you haven't even called her. What are you doing with those criminals? We thought you were locked up. Everyone saw you being taken away from the university."

He stayed standing in the middle of the living room, the mask in hand. I lowered my voice, hurried over to the wall, and pressed my ear to it. La Mariscala and her troupe hadn't returned. Not everything was lost; at least they hadn't heard us. I could hide here for a few more days while I worked out my next move. When I turned around, a wave of exhaustion swept over me, even greater than what I'd felt when I pushed Aurora Peralta off the balcony.

Santiago looked at me, almost as wild as I was, his eyes dull. He looked at me like someone who has been lost a long time in a far-off land. For the first time since I'd known him, I saw what looked like defeat in Santiago. The economist whiz kid who knew everything and could do anything had vanished. He looked like an old man. His face was screwed up, his skin full of scabs from past wounds. He was so skinny I could see his veins running over the small amount of muscle that covered his bones. He was wearing tattered jeans and a red shirt that had the eyes of the commander printed across the chest.

"Santiago, you're not going to say anything?"

He raised his hands to his forehead and grabbed his dirty hair, full of grease and dust.

"Adelaida, I'm hungry."

I went to the kitchen and came out with what was left of a loaf of bread, two or three slices in an almost empty bag, as well as some soda crackers I found at the back of the pantry and three cans of tuna that Aurora Peralta had left on the microwave. Santiago chewed hard. He pulverized the crackers between his teeth and slurped the sunflower oil from the can of tuna. I opened a beer I found in the fridge. It tasted glorious.

"There are a few bananas, if you want."

The only reply was the sound of a clump of bread being swallowed forcefully.

After peeling them, he gulped down the dwarf bananas, drank what was left of the beer, and took a crumpled cigarette pack out of his pocket.

"Can I?" he asked, almost timidly.

"What difference does it make? The smell of trash indoors and out makes it all the same to me."

"You don't smoke?"

"Not anymore but leave me the last two puffs."

Santiago smoked pinching the filter between thumb and forefinger. Only after a while did he offer me what was left. He passed it to me as he exhaled two columns of smoke through his nose.

"When they took me to La Tumba, they dumped me inside a windowless cell with no ventilation for a whole month. At first I was alone. Then they brought two more from the university. Every two hours someone from SEBIN would appear, the military intelligence guys they let loose in the marches to carry people off. He would choose one of us and shove whoever down the corridor. He'd then bring us back after an hour, beaten up and with our balls turned to jelly."

I started inspecting my hands. I felt incapable of looking him in the face.

"They didn't want to know if we knew each other or were organized. They just hit us. Time and again. We're gonna kill you, cocksucker, we're gonna rape you, we're gonna finish off your family, you fucker. Who forced you into this? They shoved a tube up the youngest prisoner's ass. The barrel of a gun up mine. They wrenched it around, enjoying themselves. Sorry for not sparing you the details."

I didn't answer or move. I tried not to look up. Was I the first person he'd told?

"In two days, they gave us four rounds each. Then they straightened us up a bit and took photos of us with a phone and shut the door again. They always made sure to hit us on the body, leaving our faces unbruised, mostly, so they could pretend we weren't being mistreated. I imagine those are the photos they sent to Ana."

I nodded.

"And they charged my sister for them?"

I nodded again.

"What did they promise her?"

"That you'd eat."

"Only that?"

"And it was a proof of life." I went quiet for a moment. "They say terrible things about La Tumba."

"All true. They stripped us naked and put us in white rooms, the only ones that had vents. It was their best torture: the air-conditioning. They turned the thermostat as low as it would go. We got fevers. We lost all sense of time, hunger, temperature. At first we shouted a lot. We started out asking for a lawyer and ended up begging for water. They brought us glasses with a broth that tasted like toilet water to me. The blows wear you down, dehydrate you, dry out your mouth and make it pasty. They hit you to exhaust you, break you. Fear makes you lucid and the blows make you stupid. That first week they always hit us separately. The next, they put us all in the same room. They pulled down our pants and made us dance. Then touch each other's balls. By this stage, we weren't completely aware of what we were doing. The worst was when they'd speak about my sister."

"What would they say?"

"That they knew where she lived. That they were going to rape her. Kill her. Both her and Julio. They knew their names. They made me beg forgiveness, but it made no difference because they'd hit me again. There were women with us. Some of my economics classmates were arrested the same day I was. Some had never protested before. We told them that marching at the front of the demonstration wasn't the same as marching in the back. But they didn't care."

"Were they hit too?"

"All of them were raped. When they took us to 'the refrigerator,' we'd hear their screams. In the other cells, the white ones, it was impossible to see or hear anything. We were isolated and had no light. We started to lose our minds. That's what it was about, making us forget the days when we were human. After a month they took us out of La Tumba to an office. We arrived wearing blindfolds. They put a document before us that accused us of half a dozen crimes: rebellion, conspiracy, instigation to commit an offense, arson, damages, terrorism. Most of us arrested that day hadn't resorted to violence. Many of the ones still locked up hadn't even been in the main body of the protest. They arrested them after they'd left the march, when they were on the way home. They waited until they were alone to make it easier to carry them off."

"Santiago, who was laying the charges against you?"

"I don't know. We asked for an officer, a lawyer, a judge, anyone to be present when they took our statements. There was no response, and no one appeared. It was a summary proceeding of the Military Tribunal, they explained. 'This is what you get when you go looking for trouble,' a man wearing a green uniform said to us. The next day, they separated us and took each of us to a different place. They took me to El Dorado prison, in the south. I was there for a month. I never thought I'd miss the SEBIN. Nobody took photos of us with their phones any longer. I imagine they had more prisoners and it was enough to extort their families. We weren't even good for that anymore. Do you know if Ana kept making the payments?"

"I'm not sure, Santiago. When my mother was dying, I lost contact with everyone. Between the clinic and taking care of her . . ." He opened his eyes suddenly. "Yes, my mother died."

"I didn't know. Well, how could I know . . ." He took the last cigarette from the tattered pack and left it on the table.

"She died a couple of weeks ago."

"Who's alive today, Adelaida? Since everything went to hell, who's not dead?"

Santiago got out of the chair.

"Where are you going?"

"To the bathroom. I haven't taken a piss in ages."

I LOOKED AT THE CEILING, wanting answers. I had to call Ana to tell her I'd found her brother. Shouldn't I? Could I? I passed my hands over the table. I'd never sat down to eat at it, but now my life was elapsing over it like an unedited film. It would be better if Ana didn't hear anything about what had happened. It would do no good. The despair would drive her crazy. *Not knowing is a way of staying safe*, I told myself, trying to pluck up the courage and keep a cool head. She was my only friend. I couldn't hide what I knew, but I couldn't tell her I'd found Santiago, either.

I got out of the chair, ready to pick up the phone. When I heard Santiago flush, I sat down again.

Ana and I had become friends in our first year of studies at the Department of Humanities. We stepped into the same elevator after seeing each other in classes for several general subjects that we both happened to take. She introduced herself and then let me know, as only she could, how much my contributions in class irritated her. I used too many adverbs and spoke like a public servant, she chided. She, like her brother, obeyed the patron saint of the uncompromising, those people who, for being pains in the neck, somehow end up becoming endearing. Thanks to her influence, I corrected my habit of adding adverbs to everything I said, though this doesn't excuse her for being so high-handed.

Happy accidents brought us together: the university time-table, the subjects we enrolled in . . . But if anyone asked me why we'd stayed friends so many years, I couldn't really give a good reason. The same thing happens with couples and marriages. Not much room for choice and if, by chance, the company is pleasant, it's welcomed. We were both reserved and a little standoffish. Unlike most literature students, we didn't feel it was our calling to overhaul national literature. We devoted ourselves to professional editing. To making the writing we worked on clean and precise, nothing more.

"And what about you?" she asked me one day in the university cafeteria.

"Me what?"

"Do you send novel manuscripts to contests and that kind of thing?"

"I'm not interested."

"Me neither," she answered and let out a raspberry sound, and we burst out laughing.

We got our first jobs as proofreaders in newspapers that eventually folded. We saw how things changed, how the devaluations, protests, and dissent were drowned out, first in the revolutionary ballyhoo, then in systematic violence. We witnessed the best years of the Commander and then the slow ascent of his successors; we got to know the first iterations of the Sons of the Revolution and the Fatherland's Motorized Fleet. We saw how the country contorted into a grotesque version of itself. Then our personal problems cemented our friendship. Life brought us together through similar circumstances, until we'd been friends ten or twelve years. I know Ana well enough to be able to say a few things. Only two matters kept her awake at night: her mother, who once she was widowed started showing signs of Alzheimer's; and Santiago, her only brother, ten years younger than she.

The clearest memory I have of Santiago is from Ana and Julio's wedding. He was fifteen. He walked through the church with a combination of self-sufficiency and reluctance. He was among the best students in his school, the city's most expensive. Ana paid the outrageous fees; she did so possessed by the strange sense that she was making a gamble, as if the money she spent on his education were coins bestowed to an invisible piggy bank. "He's extremely intelligent," she often said. He was, and he was also arrogant. She had contributed substantially to his turning out that way. He placed among the top ten in the admissions exam to the university. He studied both economics and accounting. If the country hadn't committed suicide, he would probably have ended up heading the Central Bank, his sister would say. He didn't get the chance. They arrested him before he could.

Santiago came back from the bathroom, wiping his hands on his jeans. He sat down before me, grabbed the cigarette he had taken out of the pack, and started straightening it out.

"One day, a command from the Heirs to the Armed Struggle collective showed up in El Dorado. We imprisoned students were assembled in the patio. When we were dehydrated and sunburned, eight guys arrived, all of them wearing balaclavas and lugging bagful of shirts and masks like this one." He motioned at the skull mask on the table. "If we wanted to get out of there alive, we had to go with them. Nobody thought to ask where. Anyplace would be preferable to where we were."

"I didn't realize you were locked up in a regular jail."

"They did it to everyone. Sending you to El Dorado was a way of getting rid of people who were no longer bringing in money. They sent us there to die, you understand? If you wanted to live, you could never close your eyes: anyone who didn't want you dead wanted to rape you. The prisoners had rusty metal spikes that they sold to new arrivals at the price of gold. We had to be willing to attack or defend ourselves."

I tried to interrupt.

"Adelaida, let me speak." He grabbed the lighter and lit the cigarette. "Those of us who weren't born on the inside, who didn't grow up learning to slit throats to save our own necks, don't get out in one piece. That was the way it was for all of us standing in that patio," he said, expelling another thick column of smoke. "I didn't think twice, I said I'd go with the group that was leaving that day. They never gave us back our IDs. They gave them straight to the command leaders. They called out our names one by one. They cross-checked us against our IDs and assigned us a number. Mine was twenty-five. I liked it; I'm turning twenty-five next year."

I kept my mouth shut. For some time now, I preferred not to think about the future.

"What's wrong? You think I won't make it?"

"Don't put words in my mouth."

An uncomfortable silence followed. It lasted a few seconds, until Santiago went on.

"They put us onto a bus from a border municipality. We traveled for a whole night, blindfolded, our wrists tied with wire. We jolted about in our seats. Even so, I slept. The first time in weeks."

"Where did they take you?"

"When they made us get off the bus and removed our blindfolds, I saw a mountainous rain forest. At first I thought we were in the south, Bolívar or Amazonas. But from the leaders' conversations, I understood we were in the central mountain range, between Caracas and Guarenas. For fifteen days they kept us there. Everything was makeshift, and we weren't allowed to talk to anyone. They taught us basic things. To hit. To shoot. They explained to us, in general terms, the collective's rules, among them the chain of command, so we would know not to obey leaders from other cells when we came into contact. Once we'd learned the basics, the guy who'd ranted at us at the prison, who showed up every now and then, assembled us once more. Anyone who deserted or talked would have his throat slit. To show he was serious, he made an example of a guy who had tried to escape during the most recent armed action. He summoned him by snapping his fingers. The boy stumbled forward. He grabbed him by the hair and made him kneel, in the middle of the patio, before us. The poor thing wept, begged him not to kill him, and writhed on the ground, his hands bound. The guy pulled him up by the hair again. He got out a knife and brandished it slowly, making sure everyone had seen it. Then he slit his throat. 'This is what will happen to anyone who thinks about escaping or giving away any of our armed actions,' he said."

"Is an armed action what they do every night?"

"All kinds of things get given that name: lootings, protest breakups, organized invasions. They need people for those pursuits. That's why we were recruited. We don't act on behalf of the government, but under its protection. Whatever we seize fetches up in the hands of our leaders, a mixture of crooks, soldiers, and guerrillas. These people were on a different level compared to the ones at La Tumba."

Santiago's story petered out.

"Now can you understand why I was wearing that mask today?"

He looked at his cigarette stub and then at me.

"I didn't leave any for you this time, I'm sorry," he said with a battered smile. He smoothed his hair again and looked up.

"Are you sure there's no more beer?"

I nodded. My head wound was smarting again.

"In that case I know what I'm doing now."

"What?"

"Going to sleep."

AURORA PERALTA TEIJEIRO. Date of birth: May 15, 1972. Time: 3:30 p.m. Place: La Princesa Hospital, Salamanca District, Madrid Province. Father: Fabián Peralta Veiga, native of Lugo, Galicia. Mother: Julia Peralta Teijeiro, native of Lugo, Galicia. Nationality: Spanish. Reason for requesting certificate: passport application and national ID for the Kingdom of Spain. Alongside the long-form copy of the record was a letter signed by the city's consular office, a list of required material, a leaflet with the date the issuance was scheduled for, and a phone number for queries or consultations. There were two weeks to go until the appointment. The date coincided with the one-month anniversary of my mother's death, May 5.

I grabbed a clean towel and a blanket. I left them on the dining table. I went back to the master bedroom and bolted the door. I found a red binder in the top drawer of the dresser. Inside it was another birth certificate, for Julia, Aurora's mother. She was born in Viveiro, a town on the Lugo coast, in July 1954. Both the original and a copy were together with her death certificate, issued in Caracas.

Julia Peralta died just before my first trip to the border

with Francisco. I didn't go on many trips, but the first was on assignment, sent by the newspaper I was working for at the time. I was employed there as a proofreader. In time I did a lot of things besides. I would go down to print layouts to correct a caption or I would redo a news ticker, just as I would make calls to corroborate facts that the news writers had no time to check. No one else could perform such a variety of tasks for so little money. I had copy edited almost all the articles filed by Francisco, the political journalist with the greatest number of scoops about Colombian guerrilla activities. The bosses thought I was the best person to go with him on that trip, and really, who else could do it? I had to stay at the border for as long as the operation he'd been sent to cover lasted. Though I asked, my bosses weren't forthcoming with details; they only urged me to tell them my answer as soon as possible. I accepted.

When I arrived home to pack my bags, I found my mother getting ready to go to Julia Peralta's funeral.

"What do you mean, you're going to the border? Have you gone crazy? The whole area is set to go up like a match. You're not coming to Julia's wake?"

"Mamá, I can't. Please give my condolences."

My mother was in mourning. She never usually dressed in black. It made her look like she was from a village. She was, of course, but grief reminded her of that. It stuck to her skin, as if it had been dormant in her genes all the while and had suddenly come to the fore.

"Take that off as soon as you get home, Mamá," I said before I left.

She stopped still in the living room, looking down at her dress as if secretly she agreed. Her drained, expressionless face was an island of sadness. I regretted my words. I gave her a kiss on the cheek and left.

I was agitated when I arrived. Francisco was waiting in the Portuguese's café, a place next to the newsroom that all the reporters frequented, which was run by a man born in Funchal, who had a dark mustache. You could find any journalist other than the bosses there.

Francisco had arrived first. He was sipping unenthusiastically at a black coffee. We spoke little. He didn't seem to have much of an idea what I was doing on the trip, and his star-reporter airs made me feel apprehensive. He intimidated me. But there the two of us were, killing time and sidestepping that annoying habit strangers have of making conversation when what you really want is to be left in peace.

The story that took us to the other end of the country was dangerous: the kidnapping of a prominent business owner who belonged to the national elite—when such a thing still existed—at the hands of the guerrillas. His release was to take place in the Meta River area, a hundred kilometers from the border. The family had taken it upon themselves to negotiate, without much intervention from the Commander-President's regime. Even then, the government was strengthening ties with the Colombian Liberation Forces, having created an impunity corridor in exchange for loyalty and armed cooperation, as well as royalties from the Europe-bound drug shipments that they allowed them to ferry down the Orinoco River.

Francisco had been guaranteed a safe conduct, so he could accompany the military liaisons who would work to free the business owner. My job involved staying on this side of the border, ready to resolve any eventuality: from obtaining cash or fuel vouchers to redeem at the National Guard posts, to using the scanner and laptop to send the photos and story when they were ready.

"Have you ever been to the border?"

"No."

"Well . . ."

"Well what?"

"Try not to stand out. Don't talk with people too much and, most important, don't even think about mentioning what you're doing there, or why."

"Thanks for warning me not to speak to strangers. Until now that concept had never occurred to me."

"You'll thank me," he said, raising an eyebrow.

"I'm sure."

I ordered a black coffee.

"Get it to go."

"No. I want it in a mug."

The expression of the Portuguese owner, Antonio, looked unsure.

"Don't order for me, or think for me, thank you very much."

"Whatever you say, but you'll need to be quick. We're leaving before eleven. I'll wait outside."

We traveled overland for eight hours, until we reached the town closest to the Colombian border. Francisco spoke only a few times. The first to ask me which newspapers I'd work for previously. The second to say that he hadn't studied journalism either. And the third to explain why the best journalists had never set foot in a university. I wasn't wrong: he was a jerk.

I spent two weeks away from the city. In that time, I discovered that reality has a habit of ruining convictions. This was confirmed for me in two ways: the government demonstrated a capacity for sabotage far above anything we'd ever expected, and Francisco wasn't a complete asshole. I could have foreseen the first, but not the second. No doubt there are more serene, cool-headed journalists. Better photographers, perhaps. But until then I'd never come across a creature like Francisco. He did everything: both the photographs and the articles. He was always pushing the limit. He reported things precisely, and before anyone else.

When we said good-bye in the town where I would be coordinating the rest of our stay, thirty kilometers from Colombia, Francisco asked to borrow the book I'd been reading.

"Poetry shouldn't be read in one go, so take it," I told him.

He thanked me and left.

We spoke over the phone every day. He would dictate his article and I would transcribe it. Of the fourteen he dictated I retitled all of them, which meant more calls. Some were to tell me off and others were to organize the next day's session.

"I'll call you around five, and next time, please ask before you change a headline. If it's too long, check with me."

"They all fit perfectly."

"So why do you rewrite them?"

"They're confusing. If you'd read the Gil de Biedma, the book I lent you, you'd understand the importance of precision."

After ten days embedded in a camp in Villavicencio, Francisco still wasn't completely clear on the Commander-President's intentions with the rescue operation. We gave the government the benefit of the doubt, but something wasn't right. The rescue date was pushed back fifteen days. Then two more, again and again until a month went by with no news. The country came to a standstill. Everyone was awaiting the return of the business owner, heir to one of the most important Venezuelan fortunes.

We took for granted that everything would be arranged so that the leaders of the Revolution could puff up their chests about the intermediation, but things didn't turn out as expected. Francisco had to write the reverse of his great scoop. He did so rigorously and devoid of any emotion.

His was the only photograph of the kidnapped business owner's lifeless body, which the guerrillas dumped two kilometers from the border crossing, wrapped in a jute bag stained with dry blood. He'd been dead for days. They'd made the family travel all that way only to collect a corpse, after they'd paid four million dollars that ended up in the Marxist Forces of National Liberation piggy bank.

The day after we returned to Caracas, I showed up at the newspaper's photography department with a selection of Gil de Biedma's diaries.

"Take it as an apology for changing your headlines," I said.

"There's no need. Yours were better, much better. I couldn't say it at the time, but I can now."

Two weeks later, Francisco appeared before my desk.

"I'm traveling to Meta River next week and I want you to come with me."

"For as long as last time?"

"No. Only five days. No need to take so many scanners or file a story every day, but I would feel more comfortable if you came."

"Are you sure?"

"As sure as I am that it would mean I wouldn't be sending shitty headlines. The national desk editor said it would be no problem, though he added that I'd be taking their best editor."

"Sure."

"Well, don't feel obliged. If you don't want to, no problem. We'll find someone else."

"When are you leaving?"

"Next Tuesday. We'll be back Saturday."

"All right, then. I'll be there."

"Would it be too much to ask you—"

"Ask me what?"

"To bring more books for us to read on the trip?"

"I always take too many. I'll find a few books with pictures for you."

Francisco smiled. It was the first time I saw him do so. He was forty-six and I was closer to thirty than twenty. We were together for three years, the same amount of time he had left to live.

. . .

I examined Julia Peralta's death certificate as if it were a group portrait, taken by force, that captured us squashed together and unsmiling before the blinding flash of one truth only: people croak, get sick, or are killed. They place their foot in the wrong spot. They fly through the air or tumble down a staircase. People die, through fault of their own or by someone else's hand. But they die. And that's the only thing that counts.

The year that Julia Peralta left this world, I met the only person who came into my life as if he would stay in it forever.

I'd been widowed at ten and was widowed again at twenty-nine, a week before I was to marry Francisco Salazar Solano. A group of guerrillas took issue with the photograph that won him the Ibero-American Press Freedom Prize, making him pay for it with his life. It was a portrait of his informant after the guerrillas had their way with him. They'd discovered he'd been the one to leak details about how the order to kill the business owner, whose liberation the Commander-President's government supposedly had been trying to secure for months, had come from the same government. The guerrillas gave Francisco the Colombian necktie, a technique they reserved for informers: they slashed open his throat and pulled his tongue through the wound.

When my mother met Francisco, she examined him from head to toe. His height was his saving grace, she said. And it was. He was almost six feet six, distributed in a geometrical, heavy body. The first time we made love, I thought I'd broken a rib. That wasn't the case, but almost. My mother didn't like him. She disapproved of everything about him: his stubble, the years that separated us, the two kids he had from a previous marriage.

"You're an adult, you must know what you're doing," she said when I told her I was moving in with him. "You're going to live at his house? Because it's his place, not yours. And the kids are not yours, they're his. Don't be one of those birds that raises cuckoos instead of its own offspring."

I never told her, and she never asked. She knew it already. I would have gone to the ends of the earth for Francisco. Like soldiers who head to the trenches, stupefied by anisette, which is what love must taste like when there's too much of it. If I had to pick just one of the borders we crossed, it would be his skin. Francisco photographed me with the palms of his hands and the tips of his fingers. We loved each other best without words. He never showered me with them, not even to say good-bye.

I got word of his execution two days after it happened, when news tickers about his assassination started coming from news agencies. "Winner of the Ibero-American Press Freedom Prize, Francisco Salazar Solano, found riddled with bullets and with his throat slit on the banks of Meta River, a few miles from Puerto Carreño, very close to Amazonas."

A nauseating River Styx.

One of his sources gave him away. Not the one they'd killed, but someone more innocent. The boy who had taken him to the waste ground where he took his best photo, the one with snitch exactly as his executioners had left him: with his hands holding his severed head and his testicles and penis in his mouth. That was how tattletales were killed on the border. Human beings transformed into meat, which someone else would turn into a news item displayed on the newsstands the next day. The Eleventh Commandment chiseled into the stone tablet, or into the bone of a broken neck: Thou shalt not talk. Francisco arrived at the cemetery in a similar way, his necktie quite unlike the one that he never got the chance to wear to our wedding.

Mamá went with me to the funeral. She did so in silence. And like that, in silence, we returned home. Both of us were in love with dead men. Days later a witness to what had happened on the Meta appeared. Another child. They used them as messengers. The boy showed up at the national command post, looking for the captain in charge. And there, before the military prosecutors, he recounted disjointed scenes from the killing he'd been told to relay. They sent someone incapable of understanding what he'd seen, so the dark stain of death would arrive in his innocent voice.

ALSO IN THE RED BINDER, separated by a sheaf of cardboard and tucked into several plastic pockets, I found paperwork for three bank accounts, two in Venezuela and one in Spain. The deposits and transactions made it clear where Aurora Peralta's inheritance, left to her by her mother, had gone. In the Venezuelan accounts there was barely enough to cover one month of living expenses. In the Spanish one, the numbers were far from modest, a total of forty thousand euros.

I went through everything, following a trail of pin numbers, statements, and bankbooks. I found them in a sealed beige envelope. Aurora Peralta had printed her account transactions, downloaded from the internet, and underlined them with a fluorescent highlighter before filing them in chronological order. I established that every month the Spanish government deposited a pension of eight hundred euros, as well as another four hundred for disability. Both in the name of Julia Peralta. Disability? What? And why? I'd never noticed anything wrong. I inspected each drawer looking for anything else. I was convinced that Aurora Peralta kept euros in cash. Nothing could be paid in bolívares anymore. Even the underworld stipulated that kidnapping ransoms be paid in foreign currency. The stash had to be somewhere in the apartment, but where?

On the top shelf of the wardrobe, behind a box that contained a nativity and Christmas decorations, I found a wooden box covered by a black-lacquered album and another smaller one full of press cuttings: news of a terrorist attack that happened years before and several obituaries for Fabián Peralta Veiga, Aurora's father, whose birth certificate was also in her keeping, issued at the civil registry of Viveiro in March 1948. Kept in another plastic pocket was an official-looking booklet titled "Libro de Familia." Inside it, Julia and Fabián Peralta were recorded as marrying in June 1971, in the town of Viveiro, Lugo Province, where both had been born. They were married barely two years: the death certificate of Fabián Peralta was dated December 20, 1973.

All the newspaper clippings included in the album were of the same news item, published December 21, 1973: a Dodge 3700 GT weighing almost four thousand pounds, in which Luis Carrero Blanco, president of the Spanish government, was traveling, had exploded. A bomb had sent him flying in Madrid. The bakery where Fabián Peralta toiled, next to the San Jorge church where the admiral attended Mass, got the full force of the blast. ETA had set off a bomb to assassinate the politician who had been anointed by Franco to occupy the national office, and Fabián Peralta was killed by the shock wave that emanated from it. The reference to his death was published, as an aside, in an article that headed the collection of clippings and was followed by the three obituaries. That was why Julia always had the somber look of a widow, an air that Aurora Peralta effortlessly inherited. The death of Fabián Peralta had made them grow old early and remain that way all their lives.

Julia always wore dresses down to her knee. Severe clothing that made her seem older and emphasized her thick legs and ankles. Her daughter absorbed that look. As a child she was plain, and she didn't grow into any remarkable attributes as an adult. She gave the impression of inhabiting a perpetual border that was neither Venezuelan nor Spanish; neither beautiful nor ugly; neither young nor old. Destined for the place where those who don't belong anywhere end up. Aurora Peralta suffered the curse of someone born too soon in one place who arrived too late at the next.

In the black-lacquered album were several photographs. The first was of Fabián and Julia's wedding, an austere celebration. They appeared at the altar of a church with large stained-glass windows and then at a table, where the guests were raising their glasses, smiling. Another gave a full-length view of Julia Peralta's wedding dress, which was modest— no plunging neckline, three-quarter sleeves, and two long pleats in a heavy skirt that resembled a tablecloth. Fabián was wearing a business suit, with a dark tie knotted tightly around his chicken neck. Neither was laughing, or even looking at the camera.

These were followed by other snapshots, almost all of them accompanied by handwritten captions. "Honeymoon, Portugal, 1971. Fabián's birthday, Madrid. August 1971." In a photo of the young couple standing before a dining set,

Julia was wearing a dress that enhanced her growing belly. "Christmas 1971." Another showed a group of people at a table covered in plates of food. "New Year's Eve dinner with Fabián, Paquita, Julia, and grandparents. 1971."

Judging by the photographs, the Peraltas didn't travel to Lugo often. There weren't many snapshots of Viveiro. In one, dated February 1972, Fabián was smiling before a clam casserole. There were two more photographs from those early years. Fabián and Julia Peralta, dressed more elegantly than usual. He looked very erect, with his arm around his wife's shoulders. She was holding a baby. A brief explanation stated: "Aurora's first month. June 1972." Just below it, on the same date, the three of them outside San Jorge Church. "Aurora's baptism, Madrid, June 1972." There was one more in front of the facade of the same church. The little one was in the arms of a blond woman, who stood out because of a certain beauty absent in the rest of the photos. "Aurora and Paquita," read the meticulous cursive caption.

Three photographs corresponded to the summer of that year in Viveiro: one of Aurora and her father at a beach; another with Fabián holding a platter of sardines in the middle of a festivity; and one featuring the blond woman, Paquita, once more. This time she was wearing a wedding gown and smiling, holding the hand of an unremarkable man. It was the only one of those three images that had a caption: "Union of Paquita and José. Summer of 1972." There were a couple more of the "Aurora's first steps" series and another of the father lying on the lawn: "Fabián and Paquita in Guadarrama."

Something changed suddenly. Pictures taken in the year 1973 showed the same composition, but with no Fabián: Julia Peralta almost always dressed in black with Aurora in her arms. There were several more. One of people congregated around half-eaten dishes, everyone except Julia smiling. "Madrid 1974." Paquita was present in almost all the group photos of the period. I assumed she was Julia's or Fabián's sister. In one she appeared dressed in a regional costume with a small girl in her arms. "Paquita and María José 1978." There was a photo of Julia Peralta from the same period. It stood out compared to the rest, its tone severe. She was dressed as a cleaner, with a gray skirt and a starched white apron. She was wearing her hair up, in a hairnet-covered bun. Next to her, seven women were dressed the same way. "Welcome to the new employees of the Palace Hotel, Madrid 1974."

A blank piece of cardboard faintly outlined with a date separated the rest of the photographs, which corresponded to the Venezuelan chapter. In them, Julia Peralta, a little more filled out and no longer in black, appeared in the old wooded area of Acacias Park. There were three more in Los Caobos Park. Another in front of the La India statue, in El Paraíso, and one of the modern metallic structure by Alejandro Otero in Plaza Venezuela; none of its aluminum vanes were left now, all had been stolen. Another photo: Julia Peralta, standing behind an enormous paella. Aurora's mother was smiling, the first time she looked natural in all the portraits I'd seen. In her right hand she was holding an enormous wooden spoon. Rómulo Betancourt, president of the republic between 1959 and 1964, one of the founding fathers of democracy, was beside her. Beneath the photo, a handwritten line explains: "At Don Rómulo's birthday. Caracas 1980." Many other snapshots were included in the album.

In one of them, Julia and her daughter were posing at the doors of La Florida Church in 1980. At the end of the album, slotted into four cardboard photo-corners, were a few postcards signed by Paquita, who didn't stop sending them until the year of Julia's death.

I'd gone through drawers looking for money only to discover the overlooked life stories of women I'd lived alongside, wall to wall, for years.

Inside the wooden box that I still hadn't looked through, I found an envelope full of letters. Almost all of them were written on onionskin paper between the years 1974 and 1976. Julia had signed them; they were meant for Paquita. In the first, she told her about the trip to Caracas from Madrid, in the autumn of 1974, and her arrival in a country that in her eyes was implausible. "The cockroaches weigh a pound. We live in an area that has a lot of trees. There are macaws and parrots, and every morning they come to eat on our balcony. We've found a place to live for a reasonable price." As well as her domestic notes, almost all of them related to everyday happenings, Julia dedicated some more substantial observations to the country she was making a home in, where the sun shone year-round and people could find jobs. In the Venezuela of that time, all European immigrants found jobs.

Julia's descriptions were brimming with details, such as the color and smell of the fruit, the width of the streets and the highways. "The houses here are bigger than in Spain and everyone has household appliances. I've bought a blender. I've made liters of gazpacho with it, and we store it in the fridge to drink at lunchtime." That was one of the things that Julia Peralta mentioned most: how many different things there were to buy, the same things that my mother gazed at in an appliance catalog from Sears, the enormous department store where we spent Saturday afternoons after eating an ice cream at the Crema Paraíso ice creamery in Bello Monte.

In the next letter, a month after her arrival in the city, in December 1974, Julia told Paquita that she got in touch with the nuns of a university residence "for young ladies" in the El Paraiso neighborhood, and that they had accepted her letter of recommendation from the head chef at the Palace Hotel. "Mother Justa is just as you said she would be. Very kind and devout. She hasn't lost her Galician accent after ten years here, and she tells me that, if I like, I can be in charge of the residents' kitchen."

When I was poised to read the next letter, I heard La Mariscala and her crew coming back. They slammed the door shut and turned up the speakers with the never-ending reggaeton of the previous days. "Tu-tu-tu-tumba-la casa mami, pero que tu-tumba-la casa mami." How could anyone have set the word for grave to a catchy harmony? "Tu-tumba." I pressed my ear against the wall; it sounded like there were more people than previously. The women's voices multiplied and echoed above the sounds of the music.

I returned the box and albums to their place, trying to leave them in the same order, a gesture that now strikes me as absurd. Who was going to check and confirm and verify that everything was intact? I was acting as if Adelaida and Julia would return at any moment to demand what was theirs.

I looked for a good hiding place for the red binder. Just the boisterousness of La Mariscala and her troupe granted them a power they didn't really have. My fear made me think they could travel through walls and see whatever I was or wasn't doing. I was terrified. A young man I knew nothing about was sleeping beneath the same roof I was. Santiago could be anything: a martyr, a killer, an informant. In that bedroom, which was not my own, I realized I was utterly alone. I had to do something, and quickly. I looked around at the bone-colored walls and saw a reproduction of Murillo's *La Inmaculada*, the same one my aunts had in the Falcón guesthouse master bedroom. I went over to it and took it down. When I turned it around, an envelope sealed with sticky tape fell to my feet. It was full of twenty- and fifty-euro bills.

I N LA ENCRUCIJADA, between Turmero and Palo Negro, rose a rusty metal silo stamped with the acronym P.A.N., which stood for National Food Products, which everyone identified with processed maize flour, a product that for decades fed the country thanks to all our arepas, hallacas, cachapas, hallaquitas, and bollos. Grain for the flour was stored in the Remavenca plant, visible from the bus when there was still about 125 miles left until Ocumare de la Costa. It had been the granary of Aragua State, where my mother was born; besides rum and sugarcane, Aragua's most important product was that flour, commercialized in yellow packets illustrated with the face of a woman with red lips, giant earrings, and a polka-dotted headscarf. A local, rural version of Carmen Miranda, the actress whose song "South American Way" ushered her to 20th Century-Fox studios and into the kitchens of all Venezuelan homes.

P.A.N. flour nourished thousands of men and women, until the second wave of hunger and shortages saw it disappear from the shelves and become a luxury item. True democracy dwelled in that industrialized flour. Whether rich or poor, everyone ate that starch, which was baked into so many of our memories.

The idea for the industrial production method was born from the hops with which a German brewer quenched the agonies of a country that swung from drunken binges to bouts of war. It revoked the need for *piloneras*, women who hulled the maize by driving a stick into a thick wooden mortar carved from the same tree that shaded many a hacienda's patio. From that activity were born the *cantos del pilón*—pestle songs—prayers of sweat and rhythmic blows, with melodies that accompanied the sweet and powerful grinding. Unhappy women pulverized, beat by beat, the maize hull, making the flour that wood-fire ovens would bake into the daily bread of a country still stricken with malaria. Ever since, their music has been the nation's heartbeat.

Almost always, two women would pound the mortar, chatting rhythmically. That was how the songs arose, seeming to confirm one truth: tragedy was a given, like the sun, like the trees laden with sweet, heavy fruit. The cantos del pilón preserved the grievances and stories of the uneducated women who pounded their disappointments against a wooden mortar, and some of those lyrics came to me whenever I passed by La Encrucijada.

"Adelaida, hija, wake up. We're almost at the Remavenca plant."

My mother didn't need to tell me; my heart had already detected the powerful smell of barley and nourishment. The aromas of beer and bread made me happy. So I started singing the verses I'd learned from the old ladies of Ocumare.

"Pound that pestle . . . ee-oh, ee-oh."

"So hard it breaks in two," my mother answered softly.

"You and your ma are sluts . . ."

"Not that bit, Adelaida, don't say that!"

"Your aunt and grannie are whores, ee-oh, ee-oh . . ." I said, laughing.

"No, hija. Sing what your aunt Amelia taught you: I've got a thumping headache, ee-oh, ee-oh, it's this pestle pounding I guess, ee-oh, ee-oh, but I want to fatten a pig and buy a dress, ee-oh, ee-oh . . ."

The town's black women intoned those lyrics as they stood behind the boiling skillets at the market, their hands molding the arepas. Each phrase was accentuated with gasping pants, "ee-oh, ee-oh": the groans of their exertions.

Up there on that hill,
ee-oh, ee-oh,
go the newlyweds
ee-oh, ee-oh,
Good old long neck went and tied the knot with
    donkey head
ee-oh, ee-oh.
If all this is because of your husband,
ee-oh, ee-oh,
hold onto him if you know what's best,
ee-oh, ee-oh,
he's slipping away from you but he's yet to give me a
    wedding dress,
ee-oh, ee-oh.

They sang wearing scarves wrapped around their heads and exhaling cigarette smoke. They expelled, like a lament, a lineage of females whom the world had given only arms to feed the offspring that spilled from their crotch, always torn to pieces from giving birth so often. Rocky women, with stale-bread hearts and skin made leathery from the sun and the heat of the fires and grills. Females who sprinkled their arepas with the sweet anise of their sorrows.

> There goes devil face,
> ee-oh, ee-oh,
> a demon to the core,
> ee-oh, ee-oh,
> whose tongue's gone black from the lies he's told
>   before,
> ee-oh, ee-oh.
> I don't want a married man,
> ee-oh, ee-oh,
> who stinks to high hell,
> ee-oh, ee-oh,
> I want me a bachelor who smells of ripe pineapple.

There were cantos for every trade, for practices that died out when, beckoned by the call of petroleum, country folk moved to the city, leaving behind the work melodies that had situated them in the world: melodies for milking, irrigating, grinding, grilling. Among the saddest was the *canto del trapiche*, which described the process for extracting sugarcane, sweet, dry sticks that fell off the trucks that came to

Ocumare from the Aragua valleys. I sucked on them, hiding beneath the dining table at the Falcón guesthouse. If my mother found out I'd been sucking on sugarcane, I was done for. The concentrated glucose in the earthy stem that weakened the stomach, just as rum did to rough men's brains. Bowel movements as a soul binge. The purging of everything we were carrying in our blood and heart.

The cantos de pilón were women's music. They were composed in the silent moments when mothers and widows whiled away the hours, those women who expected nothing because they had nothing.

> *Yesterday I saw you go by in a hurry,*
> *ee-oh, ee-oh,*
> *I said to my friend there goes that brazen hussy,*
> *ee-oh, ee-oh.*
> *Don't call me brazen,*
> *ee-oh, ee-oh,*
> *I'm upstanding as can be,*
> *ee-oh, ee-oh,*
> *and who are you to come round here insulting me,*
> *ee-oh, ee-oh.*
> *You and your ma are sluts,*
> *ee-oh, ee-oh.*
> *Your aunt and grannie are whores,*
> *ee-oh, ee-oh.*
> *What choice did you have when your family's got*
> *   them galore,*
> *ee-oh, ee-oh.*

> *The silly tart thinks,*
> *ee-oh, ee-oh,*
> *that her shit doesn't stink,*
> *ee-oh, ee-oh,*
> *and she lives in a house that's just a big old pile of*
> *   sticks,*
> *ee-oh, ee-oh.*

My aunt Amelia, the rotund one, sang it to me, letting out bursts of laughter in the kitchen, swearing me to silence in the event that my mother caught us. I repeated after her, like a sad, skinny parrot, my arms and thighs not a pinch on those of the large black woman beside me, that cathedral of firm flesh that sang standing before the skillet. The kind of crying that resembles a burning field.

I opened the window and peeked out at our treeless street, somehow discerning the smell of maize bread amid the deathly clouds of smoke. I closed my eyes and inhaled deeply the remains of a life story turned into a pile of sticks. Life was what had already gone by. What we did and didn't do. The platter on which we were cut in half like a bread bun about to rise.

D O YOU MISTRUST ME that much? You slept with the bedroom door locked."

"Good morning, Santiago. I slept well, thanks for asking. And please lower your voice; the longer the invaders next door take to detect my presence, the better. Oh, and the towel I left on the table is for you. Take it."

I went back to the balcony. The smoking barricade was in the same spot. No one had bothered pushing aside the Dumpsters or cleaning the plaza, which was still full of obstacles—blocks of cement wrenched from the pavement, broken bottles, sticks.

Aurora Peralta was no longer Aurora Peralta. In the place where I'd left her was a charred pile.

Everything is all right, I thought.

I peered out the window longer than usual, as if coming into contact with the outside air had made me shut down. On the asphalt were bloodstains and broken glass. Above, in the direction of La Cal, coming down Avenida Panteón, was a group of the Fatherland's Motorized Fleet. There were more than thirty of them. They advanced in a zigzag. They had megaphones and shouted the usual:

"They shall not pass! They shall not return! The Revolution lives on!"

Yes, it does live on, over others' dead bodies.

"What are you thinking about?" Santiago jolted me out of my daydream.

"The quickest way of getting you out of here," I answered, not looking up.

The direct, aggressive way he had of asking things annoyed me, as did his decisive spirit, which made me think of a leader scoping a situation.

"Look for a place to hide," I continued.

"I can't."

"Yes, you can. And you will. Not right now, but you have to soon. Call Ana, a friend, I don't know—"

"I have nowhere to go."

"I don't either. That lady crossing the road doesn't either. The thousands of people driven crazy and trapped in this city don't either. One of your university friends could take you in for a few days."

"Ah, of course, you're right, chica. All of them must be out of El Helicoide. No, no, wait! I've got a better idea! I should report to the head thug of Negro Primero. He'd be thrilled to hear how I got disorientated and lost my way, and that was why I didn't reconvene with them yesterday."

He searched his pockets for another cigarette. They were empty.

"But, sure, since they know I keep to myself and have my wits about me, they wouldn't even begin to suspect I said anything to anyone. The command will realize what happened and will intercede for sure, so the commanders don't put a bullet in my head."

He ground his teeth. He looked at me with the coffee-colored eyes of a bright boy, a chastened version of the Lasalle-educated adolescent I'd known: tall and thin like a pole for knocking down mangoes; his chin and jaw well defined; his expression lean and arrogant; his physique that of an adult, though this was not entirely complemented by a grown-up air. The fact that he was Ana's younger brother meant he was mine too. For that reason, I felt I had the moral authority to slap him. If I didn't, it was only because others had hit him enough.

"Santiago, quit it. Now's not the time for sarcasm."

"You're giving me lectures? What about you, Adelaida? Huh? Why don't you tell me what's going on? This place isn't yours, it's not your family's. There's not a single book here and you don't even know where the glasses are exactly. What were you doing in the middle of that mess? You don't have the look of someone engaged in urban warfare and the resistance. What happened? Why were you running like crazy? What were you looking for? What were you disposing of? Your expression stood out, even in the midst of all that chaos. Lucky it was me who got to you first, before somebody beat you up for real, or shot you with a pellet."

"Shhh. Keep your voice down! You did that because you wanted to. At this stage of my life I've more than demonstrated that I can take care of myself, much better than you can. I have no intention of explaining anything to you. I'm old enough not to answer to anyone, especially a boy with airs. I know you have nowhere to go, that you've been through hell. I know that. But you need to know something too: you say we're in it up to our heads. All right then, in that case all of us need to start bailing out the shit. Start by going to your sister's house as soon as possible. You can stay here two days; sleep, because you need it; clear your head. But then you're out of here. Life didn't give me children of my own, and you're not going to be my first, okay?"

In the hours we'd spent together, I hadn't seen the look of shock and bewilderment that was now on Santiago's face. He fixed his eyes on the floor and crossed his arms over his chest.

"Okay?" I repeated.

The silence stretched out until it felt stifling.

"Okay, Adelaida. Okay."

"All right then, I'm going to the kitchen. Now I'm the one who's hungry."

I opened Aurora Peralta's old china cabinet, one with glass doors, shelves, and cutlery drawers. Piled in two towers of soup bowls and dinner plates was an assortment of La Cartuja chinaware that was a little more comprehensive than ours. The look of fine bone china was evident in several dishes that our set lacked, which, arranged as they were on the shelves, had the look of an event: the tureens, the coffee cups, the platters. I took out one of the plates and examined it carefully. It seemed more ornate than what I was used to, making me doubt the authenticity of the chinaware that my mother had stored so carefully with the idea that it was valuable. I never really believed that we Falcóns ate off the same plates that Amadeo de Saboya had requested for the Royal House of Spain, but on seeing these dishes I suspected that the Peraltas were the ones who owned the authentic La Cartuja chinaware.

I wanted to feel like a real person, and eat from a plate like this, and use cutlery. Though circumstances had turned me into a hyena, I still had the right not to behave like one. And one can eat carrion with a knife and fork.

I opened more drawers. I found several cans of fruit, flour, pasta, and bottled water. Coffee too, and sugar, powdered milk, and three bottles of Ribera del Duero. There was enough canned tuna for a week, and the same went for the roasted peppers and olives. The diet of a Spanish household, remarkable in a city where there was not even bread to be had.

In the refrigerator were half a dozen eggs, a half-eaten jar of guava marmalade, and a tub of spreadable cheese. Some tomatoes and onions in a good state too, and, in the freezer, six pieces of meat on Styrofoam trays. I felt an uncontrollable impulse to eat a juicy steak, something bloody to satiate my deferred hunger. I hadn't eaten for two days. I started to weaken. Then I remembered La Mariscala and her deputies, who would react instantly at the smell. Though I guessed they wouldn't be hungry, given that they had the bags and boxes of food that the government distributed to its acolytes.

I peered into the living room. Santiago was still there.

"Come on, let's eat. There's no beer, but there's wine."

He had his back to me. He was silhouetted against the light from the window. He seemed like a ghost. His head was lowered, and his back was hunched.

I went back to the kitchen. I took out the tomatoes, the canned tuna, and two eggs to boil. In a drawer I found a dozen white tablecloths, perhaps from Julia Peralta's old eatery. I spread one of them on the table, like a declaration of peace. I took two wineglasses from an odd set and uncorked the Ribera. I went over to Santiago, who was still looking at his shoes. He got up and went over to the table. I served the wine and took a seat. After gulping down his glass, he asked after Sagrario, his mother.

"Do you know if she's any worse?"

"Up until a few weeks ago she was the same, in a world that's no longer her own or ours," I said, and he sighed. "Look on the bright side: at least she's not aware of this mess. She doesn't fully comprehend that you're not around."

"She doesn't remember me?"

"Santiago: your mother doesn't even recognize Ana anymore. And Alzheimer's with no medication makes for complications."

"How's my sister taking care of her?"

"I ask myself the same thing. If Ana hasn't gone crazy in the past few months, it's because of the steamroller effect of everything. Here, you can't go backward. You have to keep moving forward, and quickly, or you fall apart."

He gazed at his glass. He asked me how my mother had died. When I told him cancer, he knit his brow.

"And how did they give her chemo? There are no reagents. There's nothing."

"I bought the chemotherapy treatment on the black market, never really sure that I was being given the right medications."

"That sucks," he said, not lifting a finger from the tablecloth.

"What out of everything, Santiago? Cancer, the government, the shortages, the country?"

"That nobody was here to help you."

"My mother and I were used to getting by without worrying about it too much."

I went to the kitchen and painstakingly dished up the tomatoes and tuna on two plates. I wondered how we would stock up on food and water if we were locked in here. Santiago couldn't be seen, and though I could be, I had no intention of leaving him alone in the apartment. I had to search it top to bottom first. And I still had a lot to go through. La Mariscala and her invaders were also a problem. My strategy of silence was worse than an invitation to storm the apartment.

Santiago pulled me out of my thoughts.

"You know something, Adelaida? I don't remember you when you were young."

The comment threw me. I grabbed one of the boiled eggs and started shelling it.

"Are you calling me old?"

"No, it's just . . ." he labored over his words, as if to gain momentum. "I don't have any memories of you when you were at university with Ana. I remember you after her wedding. I'm not sure why, Ana spoke about you all the time."

"About you too, Santiago. For her, you were a little genius and she had to give you everything. I hope you know how to thank her someday."

"The photographer you were with the day of Ana's wedding . . . why did they kill him in the way they did?"

The expression sounded clumsy to me, though it was accurate. "In the way they did": slitting his throat open and pulling his tongue through the wound. I had trouble responding.

"He reported things that were damning for the government, and they couldn't forgive that."

"I'm not sure why I asked. I'm sorry."

The buzzer sounded. Santiago looked in the direction of the wooden door. I brought my finger to my lips.

"Don't say a word. Don't do anything. Don't move."

I started playing with the broken eggshell, crushing it against the tablecloth. It sounded once more. A ring that went on for years in our heads. In that city, the sound of the buzzer meant nothing good, especially in the situation we were in.

Ten minutes went by without us saying anything. We heard footsteps in the corridor. I peered through the peephole in the door. I saw three men dressed in regular clothing: they weren't wearing any kind of uniform, no red shirts of the Sons of the Fatherland or dark vests of SEBIN, no olive-green uniform of the National Guard. They did look like criminals, though. One of them, who seemed to be the leader of the expedition, stopped before the apartment door. "Not that one, Jairo. This one," said one of the others. "Shut the fuck up," he spat, and turned to the door of my old home.

He pressed the doorbell, which we heard through the wall of the dining room. I was scared. Santiago was a problem. And he knew it.

When I heard the scuffing of flip-flops made by whichever woman was heading for the door, I was even more afraid. What was this visit? And what did it mean? Were they coming to invade the apartment they thought was empty? Were they coming for Santiago? The dark corridor meant I couldn't make out much. With both hands resting on the door, I was filled with the sensation that I was stopping a train. I was placing my body in the path of the locomotive of the Revolution. The enemies of progress had derailed, and they were headed straight for us.

Santiago came over to the door. He asked me, bringing his hands together, to let him see. If anyone knew what the people coming to cut his throat would look like, he did, so I moved aside and waited. La Mariscala came to the doorway and told the visitors to come through. She turned off the reggaeton and sent her animals downstairs, together with the two sidekicks. I went to the master bedroom. Santiago followed me soon after. I made space for him so we could both listen to what they were saying. The conversation was to the point, no mucking about. I could understand, from what the man said, that they knew about the side business the women had going on. And they didn't like it one bit. La Mariscala's reign seemed to have its limits, and this man had come to make that crystal clear. The Revolution had strata and castes, as well as lines that she had started to overstep.

"I'll put it plainly," the visitor told her. "We know your brother works in the Ministry of the People's Power for Food and Agricultural Security. We also know you're skimming some of the bags of food from the Local Supply and Production Committees. You're getting fat on reselling them and, worse than that, chica: you're not sharing the profits with anyone. That's not good."

La Mariscala didn't answer and of course we couldn't see what expression she made, if any.

"Are you listening, *mi amor*?" The man spoke in a hurry. "Everyone knows you're selling your compatriots' food to the oligarchs. We know that this is where you're hoarding it. This can't go on. The commander wanted people who would be prepared to defend his legacy, not make themselves rich. Here, what belongs to one belongs to all."

"This is mine. I grabbed it first," La Mariscala finally answered.

"It's not yours, m'hija. Get that into your head. We frown upon those who exploit the commander's memory. And you're being extremely selfish. So I'm not saying it again: either give us the committee's boxes of food and we'll leave you in peace, or the battle begins."

Santiago and I stayed pressed against the wall, looking at each other. La Mariscala's bravado had abandoned her.

"I'm not doing anything wrong, everyone does the same thing." Her tone was weaker.

"Are you going to give us the boxes or not?" he shouted.

She didn't answer.

"I'm not saying it again: if I find out you keep making money off this, you'll have no time to hide. Get it into your head, there will be no second warning!"

The silence stretched out and grew thicker. It was broken only by the sound of the door opening and the slam it made when the visitor pulled it shut. A few minutes later, some women came up. La Mariscala shouted at them.

"Pack up all this shit, we're leaving here tomorrow! You get all the bags we set aside and sell them! The ones that still haven't been distributed, deliver them today!"

"But there are so many," one of the women responded.

"You work it out then. Don't you have the list I gave you? Find it, see how many there are. Shit's going down tonight, and before then we have to get all this outside, you hear me? Get moving!"

"But we have to deliver the committee ones, the ones we can't sell," she responded again.

"I know that, stupid. Give me that paper." La Mariscala started reading. "Ramona Pérez: give her the bag of food, she's a good stick and a good revolutionary; this one, Juan Garrido, give it to him too, he goes to the marches. Domingo Marcano, no. Not even water for that sonofabitch—"

"But we've been given orders to deliver all of them."

"I don't care, chica. I don't care. Whatever doesn't get

delivered gets sold, you hear me? And it's getting late. Get a move on, while I take care of all this!"

"But *señora*," said one of her assistants. "That food is the Revolution's. That's the commander's decision to make, not yours."

"I'm the voice of the commander around here."

No one else dared speak.

Santiago and I heard the women shuffling around and dragging bulks, a flurry of activity that lasted half an hour. When they left, La Mariscala started breaking things. One by one. What must she be destroying? What else was there left to shatter when she'd already wrecked everything? Each object that smashed against the floor was a blow to my secret hope of stealing into the apartment to rescue my papers and my mother's things. I put my hands over my mouth to stop myself from crying out. Santiago tried to grab me by the arm and take me to the living room, but I peevishly struggled free. I gave the bed an imaginary kick that I didn't follow through, out of fear of being heard. They'd taken everything from me, even my right to scream.

That afternoon I wanted to have hooks for hands. To kill everyone by just moving my arms, like a mortal windmill. I grit my teeth so hard I broke a molar, which I spat in pieces against the granite floor. I swore through my broken tooth at the country that was expelling me. I still belonged to it, even if I didn't form part of it. Hate had grown inside me. It hardened, like a spike in my stomach.

Santiago came back to the bedroom with the wine bottle.

He took a long swig. When he passed it to me, I did the same. We drank in silence, united by a new thing in common.

"Do you still think I'm one of them? Tell me, do you think I'm capable of something like that?"

I took the bottle from his hands and drank the last mouthful.

"I'm exhausted, and I'm scared, Santiago."

He nodded. "Me too, Adelaida."

We were afraid.

Much more afraid than we could bear.

I WOKE TO GUNFIRE. It sounded the same as the night before, bursts of pellet shots mixed with explosions here and there. It took me a few moments to work out where I was. I had no shoes. I was wrapped up and tucked between pillows. The door of the room was still closed. I got up and ran to the dresser. I opened the bottom drawer. The documents and money were intact, wrapped in bed linen. I looked at myself in the mirror. My face was puffy, I looked bloated. Transformed into a toad, I went to the living room.

Santiago had tidied and cleaned everything.

"They've gone."

"I know," I responded, rubbing my eyes.

"Let's go. I can get us in there without busting the door."

"Do you think . . . ?" A ray of crazy hope lit up my mind.

"No, Adelaida, they'll be back. Didn't you hear that guy? If you want to retrieve anything, now's the time. With the mess they're likely to have made, I doubt anyone will notice we've been inside. And if they notice, believe me, the last person they'll suspect is you."

His reasoning was sound. We went out to the corridor looking every which way. Santiago was holding a meat knife and a coat hanger. He used the steel blade to work open the lock and the hook to pick the deadbolt. The door swung open.

There was a strong stench of shit, and half the furniture was gone. The boxes of my mother's clothes and notebooks were sprawled all over the room. La Mariscala had broken everything: my computer, the dining table, the toilet bowl, the basin. She'd wrenched the lightbulbs from every lamp and she left her shit wherever she pleased. The home I'd grown up in had been turned into a filthy pit.

I grabbed a black plastic bag and put the sole surviving plates in it, as well as my mother's graduation photo and another two of her with my aunts in the Falcón guesthouse. Santiago was standing guard by the door.

I opened my wardrobe. Not even a T-shirt was left. I looked for the small binder hidden below the shoe rack and got out the house deeds and legal documents: my passport and my mother's death certificate. The desk was full of half-burned candles, and a few decapitated saints had taken the place of my manuscripts, which had vanished. I breathed in the greasy stench of latrine. I noticed a tower of boxes. They were sealed and labeled with the names of the people they were meant for: El Willy (Negro Primero Frontline), Betzaida (Barrio Adentro Frontline), Yusnavy Aguilar (La Piedrita Revolutionary Collective) . . . invented names, gaudy, vulgar relics of English words, their owners' attempts to concoct a refined version of themselves. The fools weren't going to get a gram of coffee, not even a bag of rice from their subsidized food boxes. The Revolution that set them free stole from them in every way possible. The first basic thing to be stolen, dignity, was followed by La Mariscala's handiwork, when she snatched their food baskets and sold them on the black market to earn double or triple, at the expense of this bribery disguised as charity. I was relieved to know I wasn't the only one they plundered. I was pleased to know that in this empire of trash, everyone stole from everyone else.

The library was deserted. What the hell had they done with my books? So many were gone. Where had they taken *Children of the Mire*, *The Green House*, *Family Airs*, *Ask the Dust*? I only had to go to the bathroom to realize that entire sections of my Eugenio Montejo and Vicente Gerbasi editions had been used as toilet paper and blocked the pipes. In silence I said to myself, running my tongue over my broken molar: *Now's not the time, Adelaida.*

Crying counted for nothing.

I looked at the bag I'd put everything in and glanced around the room one last time. My mother and I were the last inhabitants of the world that fit inside these walls. Now both were dead: my mother, my home. My country, too.

We left, not saying anything, keeping it that way until we closed Aurora Peralta's door.

Santiago appeared with a toolbox he'd found beneath the sink. With a few screws and a small metal bar he reinforced the latch and added two more locks.

"This won't stop anyone, but it can't hurt. If those women don't come back, will you move back into your apartment?" he asked, driving a screw into the timber.

I stayed silent a few seconds.

"I'm not staying here long, fifteen days tops."

"Will you be able to put up with all this for two weeks more?"

"I'll have to," I snapped.

I didn't know exactly what was combusting in me: if it was my bad mood, the fear of not knowing what to do, or the suspicion that Santiago was trying to include himself in my plans, whatever they turned out to be. Perhaps the three things together had darkened my state of mind. Meanwhile, he was attaching more locks to the door, screwing and loosening pieces with a screwdriver.

"This could slow someone down, but it's not enough to keep you safe. You have to leave this place."

Outside, tear gas bombs blasted. Pepper gas impregnated the air again. I was getting used even to that: it no longer made me retch, as it had the past few days. The shouts in the street grew in intensity. I peered between the curtains. A group of young men sheltering behind wooden shields were trying to break through a National Guard barrier. The National Guard had reinforced its ranks. They outnumbered the resistance protesters. They shot their tear gas bombs at young men just a few meters distant.

Santiago crossed to where I was.

"I'm leaving tomorrow. I think you should do the same."

His determined tone seemed strange, even harsh.

"Tonight will be worse than yesterday," I said. "I'm going to the bedroom."

I went down the hall, feeling like I was leaving a trail of destruction in my wake. I opened the plastic bag and spread

162

my things across the bed. I picked up the apartment deed, which I strained to read. The daylight was fading, but I didn't want to turn on any lights, at least until I was sure the women wouldn't be back. And even after then. Who could guarantee that nothing else would happen, that another group of thugs wouldn't arrive? Who could assure me that no one would slit my throat on a corner? That I wouldn't be kidnapped? That they wouldn't be back? Nothing would ever be the same again. And I couldn't expect to escape the next bullet that tore out of a gun barrel.

I had to do something with the wild card that Aurora Peralta's death had dealt me. I could—why not? —pass as her. I could try.

In that dark room, I made my decision. There was no going back.

I SAT ON THE FLOOR, closed my eyes, and started counting the shots. One, two, three, four. Sometimes I heard five or six in quick succession; they sounded like they were coming from an automatic weapon. The bursts of gunfire were increasing. The gas bombs, too. The repression was much worse than the day before. A band of the Fatherland's Motorized Fleet started an offensive against the buildings. Windows broke in their path. The roar of the convoy's motors was the sound track to an everlasting war. Then I heard a commotion at the entrance to my building.

I looked out the balcony window, hiding behind the curtains. A group of six or seven National Guards were beating the door with their shotguns.

"Open up! Open up the fucking door! We know you're in there and we're coming in to get you!"

I turned around and looked at Santiago, who had come to the bedroom door with the toolbox in hand, his expression unsettled. He motioned to me with his chin. We ran to the kitchen window, which overlooked the building parking lot. Out the window we saw ten masked guards pass by. Neighbors screamed from inside their homes. Something was happening on the ground floor.

"There's nobody here!" a man's voice rang out.

"No, chico, there's nobody!" we heard others shouting from the windows of the building's lower floors.

"Open the door, cocksucker, open the door right now or we'll shoot it up!" responded one of the Intelligence Service agents, whom I could identify thanks to his camouflage trousers and black vest. "You've got terrorists hiding in there!"

We watched them drag out a girl by her hair. She fought back with kicks.

"My name is María Fernanda Pérez and I'm being arrested! I haven't done anything! My name is María Fernanda Pérez and I'm being arrested! I'm innocent! I haven't done anything! I'm only protesting! My name is María Fernanda Pérez and I'm being arrested! They're taking me! They're taking me!"

"Shut up, puta! Terrorist! Slug!" The soldier delivered a kick to her stomach.

They shoved four guys ahead of them too. They were the demonstrators to whom the ground-floor neighbors had given refuge during the bombings. They were being taken away handcuffed. Every time they resisted, they fell to the ground and got a new round of kicks.

"Leave them alone!" shouted the neighbors from the upper floors.

"They're protesting peacefully!"

"They're just kids! Let them go!"

"Killers! Sonsofbitches!"

"Film it, film it, film it!"

The last to leave was Julián, our ground-floor neighbor,

who walked handcuffed, dragging his bare feet. They made him move forward by whacking him with a long machete. He was wearing shorts and a sleeveless shirt.

"You're a terrorist too, you too. We're putting you in jail, and you won't be coming out for years, you hear?"

They shoved them all into a National Guard truck cage. Santiago and I didn't say anything. We didn't shout anything. We were like gargoyles.

"Tomorrow I'm leaving, Adelaida. Tomorrow," Santiago repeated.

The truck disappeared downhill. I watched until they vanished in a cloud of smoke and lead. I wanted to tell Santiago there was no rush, he could stay a few more days if he needed. When I turned, he wasn't there anymore. I went back to the master bedroom, to hide from it all, from what I'd seen that day, and the one before, and the one before that. My head was throbbing, and my body felt punished from being on alert all the time.

I left the bedroom door open. If Santiago was going to rob me, he could have done so the minute he arrived. The passport and documents arranged in order on the bed struck me as useless objects. The real world happened out on the street, and it imposed itself with absurd force. Our day-to-day had become a matter of watching on quietly as others were carried off to jail or to their deaths. We were still alive. Stiff as statues, but alive.

Hugging my knees, I sat on the floor. I felt watched. Perhaps I was going crazy. The eyes of the commander, printed on shirts or displayed on city walls, were looking straight at me. I rested my forehead on my knees and begged God to make me invisible, to give me a blanket that would shield me so that no one could know what I was thinking or feeling.

When I saw Santiago in the doorway, I jumped in terror.

"Adelaida, it's okay. It's me."

I knew it was him, sure I did, but my body wouldn't obey me. My skin was slicked with a cold sweat, and what began as a tremor turned into spasms. My heart started beating out of control, my chest constricted painfully, and my breathing went haywire. I started gasping as if choking. The more I did it, the greater the feeling of dread. "We shouldn't make any noise," I said over and over.

Santiago took me by the shoulders and steered me to the kitchen, the only place in the apartment where the smell of tear gas wasn't so intense.

"Breathe into this."

He gave me an old paper bag that smelled like bread.

"Place it around your mouth and nose. Breathe, slower. Breathe."

My anxiety started to deflate. As my terror receded, a new feeling overcame me: shame and humiliation. My chest stopped churning and pain transformed into emptiness. Santiago looked at me, not moving a muscle. The glare of the lights from the neighboring building shone in his eyes, which were a murky color. I saw a river in his pupils. I brought a finger to my lips once more. "Shhh. Shhh. Shhh." He did the same, as if he were my reflection. We went to the living room: I leaning on his shoulder, he leading me as if I were blind.

Sitting on the couch, my back straight and flat against the backrest, I felt that my lungs opened suddenly, and the oxygen started running through my veins again, giving me back my presence of mind. Santiago stroked my hair with his free hand. His fingertips worked their way through strands of it to press against the base of my skull. He made circular motions, applying light pressure, and moved to my neck and shoulders. I removed my finger from my lips. We looked at each other a long time. We touched each other's faces as if confirming we existed. We touched each other to prove that in a country that was in its death throes, no one had killed us yet.

When I woke, it was daytime. Santiago wasn't around. He had left, just as he'd promised.

I never saw him again.

THE AGENT was a practical man. He was to the point and didn't seem all that interested in why I wanted the papers. The card and passport issued in Aurora Peralta's name would cost me six hundred euros, though. The cost wouldn't be so exorbitant if circumstances were otherwise.

"You pay for speed," he said.

I asked if he wanted a coffee. He shook his head. He kept his gaze on the material I'd handed him, glancing at the passport photos and, on a blank page, Aurora Peralta's signature, which I had traced directly from her documents.

"Sure you want nothing to drink?"

The man shook his head again. Not that there was anything special in the display counter of the café where we'd met, a *chocolatería* with no chocolate, milk, bread, or cake. Only empty refrigerators, flies, and sodas piled in a refrigerator that had a Coppelia ice creams logo, a Communist brand the Sons of the Revolution had imported from Cuba. Their products hadn't circulated long. As a smoke screen, I ordered a bottle of mineral water. The agent took out a small notebook and jotted something down. Then he closed it and left it in full view.

"Go to the restroom and put two hundred euros in here," he said softly, motioning at the notebook with his lips. "Give it back to me when we say good-bye on the street."

I went upstairs to the restroom. I chose the cubicle closest to the door. As I urinated, I folded four fifty-euro bills in half and placed them between the pages of the notebook with its graph-sheet paper. I tucked it inside my handbag, washed my hands, and strolled out confidently. The agent was waiting on the street. I gave him the notebook. We went our separate ways in the middle of Plaza Revolución, which at that time of day was full of passersby.

I stopped still in the middle of the plaza where my mother used to take me on Sundays. I looked at the plain cathedral without a portico, which disguised its insignificance with a false stucco wall topped with a bell tower. Everything around that place had been renamed or had vanished. The few centuries-old trees still standing seemed more long-lived and resilient than the country. A group of soldiers dressed in the same way as the patriotic army during the Carabobo battle were paying their respects to the Simón Bolívar statue. Their outfits were cut with coarse fabric; more than uniforms, they resembled costumes. I weaved through the preachers and evangelists. I went up Esquina Caliente, where a group of men and women dressed in red shirts often congregated, spouting the achievements of the Eternal Commander over a megaphone. They were all bearing the new version of the national flag, its eighth star the regime's addition. A recouped province of their own invention. Next to the crowd of acolytes, two enormous portraits of Bolívar, the Liberator—as we called him, perhaps due to the spate of caudillo-style leadership—depicted a military and funerary scene. They were new posters, hot off the press. They contributed to a new vision of Bolívar that the Revolution hung at all public institutions, substituting the image of the luminary of independence we grew up with.

The new physiognomy included a few changes to the until-then-documented facial features of Bolívar. Bolívar looked browner, and he had acquired a few traits that no one would think to attribute to a white nineteenth-century Venezuelan. The exhumation and genetic analysis of the remains of our national hero, which the Revolution ordered removed from the National Pantheon in a ceremony more necrophiliac than political, seemed to have added a mixed-race strain to the Father of the Nation's DNA. Now he more closely resembled Negro Primero than the son of Spaniards who rose up in arms against Fernando VII. The plastic surgery that the Sons of the Nation had performed on the past had the whiff of a sham. I walked to Avenida Urdaneta with the certainty that I was poised to leave it all behind. A mixture of disdain and fear set me apart from my country. Like Thomas Bernhard in the pages of *Gathering Evidence* and *Woodcutters*, I started loathing the place where I was born. I didn't live in Vienna, but in the middle of a big mess.

Ay, garabí!

THE PROCESS of becoming Aurora Peralta had begun; it could even be said that I'd successfully crossed my first line of impersonation. I went to the Spanish consulate dressed in her clothes, three sizes too large for me. My clothing had disappeared from the wardrobe of my old apartment. I had nothing to wear, except her size 42 dresses and trousers. It took me days to grow used to my ashen look of a woman turned matron before her time. I spent hours in front of the mirror studying the small calamity of my appearance, a routine of self-affirmation where, while I didn't notice any concrete progress, I did notice utter destruction.

When I planted myself in front of the small digital camera of the consulate for the biometrics passport photo wearing Aurora Peralta's large black dress, I didn't know if I should smile or simulate the constipated look of faces on IDs. In the end I wore an unhappy, deceptive expression, going by what was printed on the document that I held between my hands.

On the consular office doorstep, I opened the booklet with the words UNIÓN EUROPEA—ESPAÑA in embossed golden letters. On it, my face was linked to an age and a territory not my own; to a story of misfortunes and joys that were foreign to me and for that reason unimaginable. Aurora Peralta's life was one I knew little about, and yet I had to submerge myself in it immediately. Faced with the long line of children and grandchildren of Spaniards all waiting their turn to collect a document that would be their ticket out of the country, I felt the good fortune of the desperate. I was not that woman; I never would be, not fully. Between the sword and the wall, one can always choose the sword. That passport was my steel, an ill-gotten Tizona.

Now isn't the time for regrets, I told myself. Things were the way they were.

It was my duty to survive.

AFTER SANTIAGO LEFT, everything took a turn for the worst. La Mariscala and her followers returned, this time with reinforcements: a troupe of another dozen women crammed into colorful leggings. They embodied an absurd fleshiness in a place where everyone was dying of hunger. Five of them occupied the empty stores on the ground floor, part of their colonization strategy. One of the stores housed the headquarters of the Mujeres Libertadoras Frontline, or so said a makeshift sign they taped to the wall. The other half of the group continued taking orders from La Mariscala. They bustled about all day in my old place, now converted into a warehouse for food boxes.

La Mariscala must have won the battle against the thug who tried to ruin her now-thriving business selling regulated food on the black market. Things were going well for her. People went into and out of the apartment at all hours. They dragged bags and packets of food, as well as enormous boxes of toilet paper. If a product was in short supply, these women had it. They no doubt charged double or triple what it sold for at the people's markets, which the Revolution set up in an effort to mask the shortages with half-empty shelves. They occupied the midpoint of the chain, were stakeholders in the black market.

La Mariscala chose our building because it was close to the revolutionary market and, at the same time, it could compete with other businesses in the area, which received almost no goods. The Sons of the Revolution accused the owners of those businesses of being hoarders. This was where La Mariscala had a captive audience: in the desert of the hungry middle class that didn't receive the Revolution's handouts. She did so through speculation. It was a practice the leaders attributed to capitalism, yet it was how she and others filled their pockets.

They rarely slept in my old apartment. They only used it to sort out their stock. Their nightly absences gave me a small window of peace. I did everything from ten in the evening: I showered, rustled up something in the kitchen, moved things, walked around more naturally; but I never turned on the light. The neighbors tried to fight them. Gloria from the penthouse was the first to organize more urgent actions. She went from door to door, rallying the neighbors to decide on a common defense strategy. On two occasions she rang Aurora Peralta's doorbell. In the dark, as if I were in a grave, I stayed mute and immobile. One day I heard her ask a few neighbors for Aurora's whereabouts, even for mine. No one could give her an answer. They didn't have one, or want to know it.

Enclosed between those walls, I devoted myself to studying and untangling the life story of the woman I had to become. The first thing I did, after going through her mother's letters and photograph albums, was charge her phone, which had three voice mails. All of them were from María José, who had written urgent emails too. I hurried to answer, explaining the motives for the silence: the riots, the blackouts, the internet service being sabotaged.

I wrote as Aurora Peralta, imitating her style. The response was immediate. "When are you coming?" "As soon as my passport's ready," I typed. That was answer enough, at least judging by the secretarial and succinct prose of Aurora Peralta herself.

Her computer was old, and it autocompleted navigation details, including passwords. I accessed all her information without a hitch. I focused on the bank accounts and emails. First, I confirmed that the electronic signature of the account in euros was correct. There were four numbers that the bank had sent to Aurora in an envelope, which she stored with the rest of the information: email passwords, email addresses, telephone numbers, and physical addresses. The four digits still worked. Once her phone was charged, and with the security key that the bank sent via text message, I managed to transfer small amounts to the credit card issued in her name but linked to an account that still identified her mother, Julia Peralta, as coholder. I didn't want to leave any loose ends. I tried to make sure that everything was in order.

The second part was more complicated: reconstructing Aurora Peralta's relationship with her Spanish family. All the emails in her inbox were from her cousin María José Rodríguez Peralta.

I had trouble building a picture, maybe because when

people know each other everything is taken for granted. María José was the daughter of Paquita, the woman I saw in the photos from the seventies, which I started studying exhaustively from that point forward. Now Francisca Peralta was eighty-one years old and, according to what her daughter wrote to Aurora, she was the one insisting she leave the country. A way of repaying the long history of outstanding accounts with her sister-in-law Julia.

I dipped into the letters that Julia Peralta wrote to Paquita. She was the one who encouraged her to cross the ocean after Fabián's death. They wrote to each other at least once a week for the first eight years. The correspondence started to space out, though Julia never neglected the monthly five hundred bolívares, or sixty-eight hundred pesetas, that she wired her in-laws. Paquita asked after little Aurora and insisted that they visit for the summer. "I know you're working hard, but you could send Aurora. We miss you, and it would be wonderful if María José and Aurora could spend some time together. They're close in age, after all."

As far as I could tell, the Peraltas traveled to Spain on only one occasion after they left. It was in 1983, when their origins were still fresh in their memory. As Julia Peralta adapted to her new country, a transformation occurred: she went from working as a cook, a job she started as soon as she arrived, to opening her own restaurant, a small tavern. Casa Peralta was a strange place, like all immigrant bars initially. Sometimes it functioned as an eatery, sometimes as a café or bar. I remember that Julia Peralta sent out a small canapé with each glass of wine, and even with sodas. The servings were generous: octopus, scrambled eggs, arroz caldoso, and paellas that sated the appetites and melancholia of those who ate there almost daily. In time, Julia Peralta put Venezuelan dishes on the menu: maize empanadas stuffed with meat and cheese, and arepas, which she offered once she employed a kitchen assistant. These additions attracted public servants from the nearby ministries, who would go there for weekday breakfasts and lunches.

Julia—the Spanish woman, as people called her—became Doña Julia. Business improved at Casa Peralta. Word of her special touch meant soon she was receiving more substantial orders. She started offering set meals for first communions and ended up cooking *arroces a la marinera* and paellas that the Social Democrats served during their electoral campaigns. It could be said that Julia Peralta fed two generations of political leaders of democracy. They won several consecutive elections, a run of almost twenty years in total, and in that time the Spanish woman found her place in the city.

She made quite a name for herself. In the restaurant dining area she hung a framed newspaper feature that pictured her in the kitchen, smiling. "The Spanish woman who cooks for the *adecos*," as they called the center-leftist politicians, the first to legislate universal voting, free basic education, and the nationalization of petroleum. Until social democracy was buried by two coup attempts, which paved the way for the Commander's political career and his Sons of the Revolution movement, Julia had been the woman who cooked for democracy celebrations, while they lasted.

My mother liked going to Casa Peralta on Sundays. She

thought it was a respectable place—something she said when relatively good taste and decorum were guaranteed. We would invite Don Antonio, who always ate alone, to sit with us. He was from the Canary Islands, from Las Palmas, and was the youngest of seven brothers and the founder of the first book distributor in the city. I liked listening to him as he talked to my mother. He had arrived toward the end of the fifties. He told us that he had to pedal up and down Bulevar Sabana Grande, selling baseball cards and science primers to newsstand owners in the area. Then he bought a pickup and took to the road to sell the latest arrivals in other cities throughout La Cordillera Central until he opened his bookshop. He called it Canaima, like the Rómulo Gallegos book.

Aurora Peralta moved about the tables, taking drink orders and leaving baskets of bread for the diners. She also served the starters, while her mother went into and out of the kitchen holding a steaming clam casserole. She was an ugly child who stood on the other side of the bar shining glasses and removing cakes and tarts from their molds with a disgruntled air.

Though she became an adolescent in Venezuela, she hadn't absorbed any of the informality and merriment that surrounded her. She was devoid of all grace and joy, as if she'd stayed impervious, mired in her own grayness. Her life story was full of gaps and unfinished episodes.

Transforming myself into Aurora Peralta was a losing battle before I'd even begun. From now on, I wouldn't be thirty-eight but forty-seven, and I had to seem like a cook with a certificate in tourism and secretarial studies to her name, judging by the unexceptional qualifications I found, not a language and literature major who specialized in editing. That involved a downgrading in social status.

What expression would I wear when I introduced myself to the women of her family? María José kept insisting that I bring forward my leave date. And she was adamant to the point of nonnegotiability that I stay at her place while I set myself up and learned how things worked in Madrid. Paquita, her mother, was elated. She wanted to see me. "It's been so many years," wrote Aurora's cousin. To pluck up my nerve, I reminded myself that decades had gone by since Aurora Peralta traveled to Spain, which would help justify my appearance. It would even be understandable if I didn't remember names or places. But I was troubled by the thought that the family could have seen a photo of the real Aurora, and even more worried by the details I'd forced myself to memorize. It would all swirl into one big soup. The risk of failure was enormous.

On top of pretending to be someone else, I had another difficulty: how to explain my disappearance from my own life. Emails from the publishing house I worked for wouldn't stop peppering my inbox. At first they only wanted to know how I was and if I had recovered enough to take on a new manuscript. The fact that editing and selling books were increasingly extravagant and ruinous activities in Venezuela worked in my favor. But the cease-fire was short-lived. The regional editor wrote to me. She was perturbed by my silence. She asked if she should consider it a rebuff. I decided my demise should be abrupt and shouldn't include too much explanation. I wrote a succinct response telling her of my decision to leave the country for a time. It seemed that the national circumstances, and even Adelaida Falcón's personal ones, were enough to convince her.

"I need to get back on my feet after my mother's death. After all the deaths," I typed.

Finally, in another dilapidated café, the agent delivered me the false Venezuelan papers I needed to leave the country as Aurora Peralta. That afternoon I bought a plane ticket to Madrid on the internet. I could have left the same week if it hadn't been for the drastic reduction in the number of international flights due to the protests that were scourging the country. I paid with Aurora Peralta's credit card. It was a relatively high sum. When I saw the sale go through without incident, I let out a sigh of relief. Money made everything quick and simple. Having it made you a target for those who wanted it, but not having it was worse. And that was how most people lived. In perpetual bankruptcy.

T HEY'D STOLEN THE VASE, as well as four letters from the epitaph. They'd wrenched the word *Descansa* from Adelaida Falcón's grave. The *en paz* remained, like a debt that no one would ever pay. Her surname was missing too, as well as the consonants from the town where she was born and where I spent part of my childhood. They had wrenched them off one by one until only extinguished letters remained, stammered like the F in Falcón in the sign at my aunts' guesthouse. For losing, we even lost our name. The Falcóns, queens of a world that was in its death throes.

I took an empty vase from another tombstone, so that the white carnations wouldn't wither in the heat of my own shame. It was a month since she'd died. And even though I was no longer the same person, I wanted to be Adelaida Falcón while I stood before her. I wanted to tell her how much I loved her. Like my mother, I was dead too. She was belowground. I was on the surface. That was why I went that day. To weld our worlds back together, talking to the wind.

I don't know how long I stayed at her grave, but it was the longest conversation we'd had. Even if there were no words left, even if we only shared this bit of lawn, it was the closest we could get to each other in this part of the world. Death happens quickly when the world insists on turning. And our world, Mamá, didn't turn until we found each other, like in Eugenio Montejo's poem. It didn't, Mamá. It tipped over and fell on everyone else. It crushed the living and the dead, binding them together as one. As for home, our home, nothing is left of it; I couldn't protect it, Mamá. You must know, too, that other things have changed. That I'm no longer your namesake, that I'm leaving here soon. I don't expect you to understand, only listen. Can you hear me? Are you there, Mamá? I came to tell you things I thought were obvious but weren't. But are not. I came to say that I never cared that my father was dead to us. Bearing your name was enough for me. It was the only roof over my head that I needed. Naming me after you, Adelaida Falcón, was a way of sheltering me. From vulgarity, from ignorance, from stupidity.

Since I was a little girl, I've felt secretly proud that you decided not to live in your hometown (beautiful and charming, but, at the end of the day, a small place, stifling). That you preferred other things besides playing bingo at the hour of the mosquito plague, besides the rum and the cinnamon guarapos that numbed the souls of everyone who lived in Ocumare de la Costa. I liked that you didn't resemble your sisters. That you were quiet and reticent. That you despised superstitions and coarseness. That you read, and taught others to do so. You seemed, Mamá, like the country I took as a given. With its museums and theaters. With its people who took care of their appearance and minded their manners. You didn't like anyone who ate or drank too much. Or those who shouted or wailed. You hated excess. But things have changed. Now everything is spilling over: filth, fear, gunpowder, death, hunger.

As you faded away, the country went crazy. To survive, we had to do things we'd never imagined: prey upon others, or remain silent; leap on someone else's neck, or look the other way.

It's a relief you didn't live to see it. And if I have another name now, it's not because I wanted to leave the country that we formed with your name and my own. I did it, Mamá, out of fear. I, as you know, was never as courageous as you. Never. That's why, in this new war, your daughter is on two sides at once: I'm one of the hunters, and I shut my mouth. I'm someone who protects her own, and someone who steals others' belongings in silence. I inhabit the worst of both camps, for no one claims the casualties of those who live, as I do, on the island of cowards. And I, Mamá, am not brave. At least not in the quiet way you showed me. You willed me bravery. I wasn't brave. Like Borges in the poem, Mamá.

I knew women who swept patios to give their lonely days a structure. You did too. An extinct race. Aunts Clara and Amelia, and those who went before them and visited us in our dreams. Paper cutout women who hung from metal hangers in the wardrobes of my nightmares. The severe old ladies from the church in Ocumare, all wrapped up in their novena and Nazarene ways. The ones who smoked with the flame *pa' dentro* and lost their teeth from giving birth so many times. Or those who appeared to the dying, fending off death saying, *pa' tras, pa' tras*. They populated a planet that's magnified, now, in my memory. Aunt Clara got up so early to sweep, do you remember? I saw her clean and scrub the cement floor of the patio, around its shrubs and twisted trees: tamarind, passion fruit, mango, mamey, cashew, geni-pap, the stone plum, martinica, guanabana. What fell from those trees was sweet and tart at once, leaving a trace of something rotten in the mouth, an excess of sugar that drove the heart and tongue crazy. Aunt Clara lived in her garden, was boss of the place where roots are planted and torn up, where life and death are equidistant. I remember her, a soldier in a nightgown who went out to slay her memories with a rake.

Our life, Mamá, was full of women who swept to give their lonely days a structure. Women in black who pressed tobacco leaves, who used a spade to scoop up the fallen fruit that smashed against the patio floor in the early morning. I, in contrast, don't know how to shake out the dust. I don't have patios or mangoes. The trees in my street drop only broken bottles. We didn't have patios, Mamá, and that's not a criticism. In the early morning, and sometimes in the middle of the night, I sweep my own patch of land until it bleeds. I gather my memories and arrange them in a pile, like we used to do with the leaves in Ocumare de la Costa before we set them alight in the late afternoon. The smell of fire exerted a secret fascination over me, but it was shattered a few days ago. Fire only cleanses those who have nothing else. There is grief and desolation in things that burn.

Since the night you talked to me about my grandmother and the eight women, her eight sisters, who appeared at the foot of her bed as she was dying, I think about us. About what we were, together. You know already, family women. Our tree with its spindly branches and fruits that never ripened fully into sweetness. You know something, Mamá? I haven't done right by our women. I haven't called Clara and Amelia since I told them you had died. I will call them, Mamá, don't you doubt that. For the moment I want to save my words. Looking back only sinks me farther into the land I must leave. Trees are sometimes transplanted. Ours can't stand it here anymore, and I, Mamá, don't want to burn like diseased tree trunks do when they're tossed on a pyre. I'm not sure I'll see Clara and Amelia again. And I'm not worried. They have each other, like we did. But that, as you can see, is of little use now. And I've come here to tell you other things.

I never told you exactly what happened. Do you remember that afternoon when I got lost? I didn't lose my bearings or get distracted, which I'm sure you always knew. I left the Falcón guesthouse to run an errand you'd sent me on: to buy a kilo of tomatoes.

"Do you know how much a kilo is, approximately? Do you know, Adelaida?"

I shrugged.

"This is a kilo."

You showed me with both hands, holding the imaginary scale that the real-world tomatoes would sit on.

"Do you understand?"

"Yes, Mamá," I responded, looking at the mango treetops.

"Pay attention, Adelaida. Concentrate: make sure they

don't give you any less. Like this, remember." You showed me with your hands once more. "They have to give you change. And don't dawdle. I don't like you wandering around town by yourself."

I walked to the market in the plaza. I asked for what you'd sent me for. They gave me a bag of small, ugly tomatoes. I paid and slipped the change into my pocket. I scanned the stalls, not overly interested. The dogfish-stuffed empanadas, right at the end, at a stall attended by a woman who was kneading kilos of flour. Those makeshift stands where huge men from the port bought empanadas by the pair. They took anxious bites and bathed them in a hot green salsa that streamed down their chins. I also went by the stall with glass jars full of baby clams and trays of sardines, snapper, and mackerel. The fish, open-mouthed, with their small teeth and their stomachs slashed, were lying on hanging scales, the needles going haywire. They smelled of innards, salt, and copper.

I also went by the ice-cream stall, where cups of shaved ice dyed with colored syrup, the frosty peak topped with sweetened condensed milk, were for sale. I went from one stall to another, my bag of tomatoes in hand.

It was hot, the heat of seaside towns. I should have gone home. It was an order, and I rarely disobeyed. Your instructions were a transfer of power within our domestic realm. They conferred responsibility upon me. They momentarily released me from the perpetual state of childhood. It was like wearing high heels, but better. That afternoon I chose to renounce the sovereignty of the Falcón republic. My excuse could be that there were a lot of customers and I had to wait, or that the trucks that brought goods from the port were held up, hindering the grocer's attempts to restock the tomatoes.

The point was to stay away. That day we were having tortoise pie, so the Falcón kitchen was bustling with matrons-cum-slaughterers. I preferred not to watch my knife-wielding aunts Clara and Amelia in their cretonne dresses, all ready to shove Pancho—the red-footed tortoise I fed lettuce leaves, now about to be cooked like any old lobster—into a pot of boiling water, after which they would chop him up and stew him with chili, tomatoes, and onions. I licked my lips just thinking about eating tortoise pie, but I preferred not to pay the price of hearing Pancho being boiled alive. All the tortoises I remember emitted a squeal that sounded human to me and reverberated in my stomach later, when I was guilty of having happily scraped my plate clean of the tasty result of their suffering. I adored the soft meat's sweet and spicy flavor, but I wanted to enjoy it without having to witness the persecution and sacrifice of that critter. Tasting the prey with no reminder of its death. Eating it guilt-free. The same thing is happening now, Mamá. I take my seat at the table, trying to forget who has carved the fillet of my well-being out of the slaughtered beast, and with what knife. That's why I was telling you about taking sides, about those who steal and those who turn a blind eye. Those who kill without lifting a finger.

That day, I walked up La Cuesta de los Perdidos, remember? The hill of the lost: the name we gave the street you'd told me hundreds of times never to visit. "Nothing good ever happens there," you'd say. In Ocumare everyone talked about that street. At the end of it was an abandoned house. The architect's house. Even my aunts and you mentioned it at times. Aunt Amelia whispered its name, horrified, making the sign of the holy cross before kissing her thumb. You took her to task. That was what uneducated people did. "Superstitions!" you brought the discussion to an end, lowering your voice.

I had no trouble finding the mansion. It was at the end of everything, almost abutting the river. The main gate, a red color, had a broken padlock and wasn't shut properly. I went in, drawn by one of the cotton plants that graced the main garden. I'd never seen anything like it. It was covered in white, spongey lumps. I felt like pulling them off and nibbling on them.

In my aunts' tone, "the architect's house" sounded like it must belong to a perverse magician, a bad man. So I was surprised to find, in that small and brackish backwater, a dilapidated but beautiful modern house with balanced, generous proportions. It was as if the Bauhaus had been tasked with bestowing order and progress on a scrubland. It seemed inexplicable to me that such dark comments could be directed at one of the few beautiful buildings in that dump. The house had nothing in common with the dark and ugly place I'd invented in my head. Its beauty redeemed everything surrounding it: the corrugated-iron houses and prefab blocks where fishermen salted and dried dogfish; the liquor stores with beaded curtains where men went in and out, swigging anisette on the plaza pavement. That house didn't belong to the town—to its world, either.

I went inside unafraid, drawn by the white fixtures and colored glass windows. But the interior was destroyed. Creepers and weeds had swallowed up the white metal and glass staircase almost entirely. The tidemark on the walls spoke of floods, and door handles had been wrenched off. The mess was a sure sign of thieves, and the corners were full of wasp nests. Only a few pieces of furniture were left, and the floor was scattered with papers: notes on the theory of additive color, jottings on how to keep a sphere in the air, as well as designs and drawings of metal structures.

I peered at the books that covered one white wall. The first shelf was full of volumes in French. It was the first time I'd seen a book from Éditions Gallimard. It looked sober and elegant to me, with its twin border lines on the bone-colored cover. I found a lot of art manuals that had their pages ripped out. I'd never read those names before. The strange sound of some of them meant that they became embedded in my memory: Josef Albers, Jean Arp, Calder, Duchamp, Jacobsen, Tinguely . . . one plate corresponded to each artist, accompanied by a long text. The reproduced artworks seemed familiar to me.

In the city, the streets and subway cars, even the zebra crossings, had a similar style. It was years before I understood that something of the brightness that shone in that forgotten house in a seaside town had scattered all over the country: it was the promise that one day we would be modern. A statement of intent. But our intentions were in ruins too, like the metal murals ravaged and looted of their original beauty by scrap-metal collectors. The bare bones of those sculptures rose all around the city. I wanted to move into the architect's house. I fantasized about cleaning it and setting it up so I could while away the spare hours that I had in abundance at the Falcón guesthouse.

A few fat blowflies flew around the main living room. Near the stairway I found a few objects that had nothing to do with the spirit of the place: broken missals, decapitated saints, coverless New Testament booklets. Also empty aguardiente bottles, seashells, chicken feathers, and dirty rags. I went up the steps, afraid and fascinated. They creaked, eaten away by Ocumare de la Costa's briny air. From the highest point I could see the cotton plants, which at that time of day were iridescent, bathed in sun. The sounds of women washing their clothes in the river drifted up to me.

The bag of tomatoes slipped from my hands and fell on an empty cardboard box, which echoed as if I'd dropped stones, not vegetables.

"Who's there?"

It was a man's voice. I scooted down the staircase and slipped over. I scraped myself badly, but my panic was greater than the burn. I ran out, not looking back, and didn't stop until I got to the market plaza. It was only then that I slowed enough to realize my pants were ripped and stained in blood.

I got back to the guesthouse an hour later. I don't remember what was worse, Pancho's squeals as he was boiled alive in the pot or the look you gave me, Mamá, when I arrived, my clothing torn and no tomatoes in sight. You didn't believe me when I said I'd lost my bearings, I know. You were angry on the inside, which is how feelings hurt most, when they fester. You went out for the tomatoes. We ate Pancho's remains unhappily. My aunts came in and out, their large, old-lady backsides wobbling.

"Amelia, it's bland," said Clara to her elder sister, who shot her a furious look.

"Put a rein on this girl, she's not keeping to the straight and narrow, Santo Cristo!" responded Amelia, thrusting her anger in another direction.

"Virgen del Valle! The girl will turn insolent," griped Clara.

You, Mamá, ignored my aunts' drama. You ate the smallest piece of pie.

"Adelaida, m'hija, I kill the critter myself and you're not going to eat it? This girl's going to sour our day. My goodness you're stubborn, child, look what you've done to your mother." My aunt Clara fixed her crazy-snake eyes on me, offended, according to her, at the upsets and the spectacle I'd made.

You, Mamá, ate without raising an eyebrow. You were the first to leave the table and wash the dishes. You didn't speak to me for two days. My first silent punishment hurt more than any hiding. But that's how you were, Mamá. That was just you.

The taxi driver honked twice. I'd taken a lot longer than the time we'd agreed on. I left, this time without looking back. Digesting the letters wrenched from our name, yours and mine: Adelaida Falcón. I got into the passenger seat, feeling emptied out. I explained to the driver the directions they'd given me in the cemetery's general office. We headed for the allotments with no hills, quadrants with graves deep inside flower beds, wherein the residents decomposed, piled on top of each other, with no view.

"Wait here. I won't take as long this time, and don't worry, I'll pay extra."

The man snorted, as if the trip would be the ruin of him. I got out and shut the door hard, a bunch of daisies in hand.

No one was in the graveyard. The long rows were covered in crackling leaves. This part of the cemetery, older than the part where my mother was buried, mostly had European immigrant graves. Despite following the same severe rectangular pattern, which made all the tombstones equal, some had small extravagances: toy windmills and candy for children who had been dead twenty years, Easter plants and little Christmas trees singed by the sun. Scores of tombstones were fitted with oval portraits of men and women dressed in old-fashioned clothing.

I found Julia Peralta's grave a few steps from a tree. A thick layer of weeds covered almost all of it. I had to kneel and pull out a few weeds to read her full name. Julia Peralta Veiga. A squadron of furious leafcutter ants pooled out in all directions. There were hundreds of the red things, which looked like the ones used to make hot salsas and season bitter cassava juices. The insects surrounded the enameled photograph of Julia Peralta, a studio portrait, charmless and cold. Julia Peralta had something of that air in life, too: as if she were beyond this world. While I tried to arrange the daisies in the vase, one of the ants bit my index finger. I jumped backward, squeezing it. It was a big bite. A pinprick that palpitated and burned. I tried to move the rest of the weeds with a stick, but it was impossible. My finger swelled in a few seconds, an allergic reaction.

Julia Peralta must have thought my visit inappropriate; that was why she drove me from her grave with an infantry of ants whose eggs multiplied at the orders of the queen. Sucking my finger like a child, I picked up the small bunch of flowers, already withered, and placed it on the cement plaque printed with her name.

I'm not sure if I was asking her forgiveness or her permission. I didn't know what I was doing, standing before the grave that, if it hadn't been for me, could have housed her daughter too. Julia Peralta slept peacefully a few meters belowground. Her daughter, in contrast, had been incinerated in a Dumpster. It was me who did that. It was me who abandoned her there. Me.

If we belong to the place where our dead are buried, which of all the places did I belong to now? The dead can only be buried when there is peace and justice. We didn't have either. That was why there was no rest, much less forgiveness.

I I I, I I I, I I I'm bringing you a bunch of flowers; they're for you San Juan, in all their different colors! Ocumare de la Costa's black residents sang on June nights. The clock keeps on ticking, you can't turn it back, bananas will never be green again once they've gone black they chanted, moving their hips on the beaches of my childhood. *I I I, I I I, I I I'm bringing you a bunch of flowers; they're for you San Juan, in all their different colors!*

I left the bunch of daisies I'd bought for a woman I didn't know well, someone I'd robbed of everything. And just as San Juan didn't return to heaven, peace didn't reign on earth. That afternoon it felt like the cemetery trees were dropping feathers from decapitated hens. Like the tomatoes were exploding again. Like the tortoise was squealing inside the pot of boiling water. Like cotton and fish were coming out of my chest. Like my dead mother was condemning me to an eternity of silence. And like my other mother, the Spanish one, was feeding ants with her body, was feeding their venom, in the land where she chose to die.

In this country, no one rests in peace. No one.

"To Avenida Urdaneta, where it meets Esquina la Pelota," I said to the taxi driver before pulling the door shut.

C ALLING PASSENGER Aurora Peralta. Passenger Aurora
Peralta, please report to airport staff."

I had to leave my Venezuelan passport on the counter. I
went down to the tarmac. I obeyed, the only option when
you have no choice.

"Dammit," I said under my breath as I adjusted the reflec-
tive vest that those of us who had something to declare were
made to put on.

It was the third inspection, so I supposed it was the de-
cider. The one that determines whether you stay or go. I was
sweating more than usual and was being overly affable, a
sure giveaway when you're not a good liar and don't know
how to commit a crime. There I stood watching how an official from the National Guard took great pleasure in ex-
ercising command, at least with me. He made me lift my
suitcase onto a metal table. He raised his hand in a signal
not to approach. He unlocked it. Click, click. He looked me
in the eyes, leveling his green uniform at me, not to mention the cluster of medals on his chest, the gun at his belt,
and the bullet holder around his waist, its bullets yet to be
premiered. This official snooped through my things as only

authority figures know how when they are busy demonstrating that they are The Authority.

"Why are you taking so many books and papers?" he upbraided me. "What do you do?"

"I'm a cook."

"That's it?"

"Yes, that's it."

He inspected the items jumbled in my baggage. My things: books, old notebooks, photos that would only serve to jog my memory about who I really was or had been, if the need ever arose. Then there were the other things: Aurora's dreadful, out-of-date clothing; the photo albums and letters I'd sifted through and studied and was now carrying with me like a student preparing for an exam. In a false bottom I'd made especially for the trip were the two apartment deeds, Aurora Peralta's and mine. Carrying them wasn't a crime, but even so, I'd hidden them.

In the middle of the tarmac of the Eternal Revolutionary Commander's International Airport, flustered by the smell of sea and fuel, I watched the items of mine that were meant to cross the Atlantic being paraded before me. It felt like I was standing in front of a whale that had been ripped open and was letting me touch its innards. I felt ashamed, wanted to cover it up and cover myself up, but I didn't protest. I didn't lift a finger. I didn't ask the official how many bullets in his holder had our names on them. Nor did I want to take shelter in the solidarity of those who were still in line: civilians forced to obey.

"So you're a cook. What kind of food? You don't need so many books to cook now, do you?" he persisted.

"I make pastries and sweets, Officer. I also like to read. I get bored waiting for the oven to heat up; that's why I read so much."

"Mmmm . . . In that case, what else . . . ?"

"I don't understand." I kept looking at him.

"I'm asking you what else you're going to do. Are you going to Spain to work as a cook? You only have a one-way ticket, citizen. I don't see the return flight anywhere here."

I went over my memorized speech, as I'd done hundreds of times in front of the bathroom mirror.

"Look, Officer, my aunt's sick. She's getting on, the dear old thing." I hated speaking like this, but it was a way of driving home the part I was playing, "and, you know, I have to take care of her. My return trip depends on when she gets better. That's why I haven't bought my ticket yet."

"Hmmm, okay . . ." he said with a simian air, as if he didn't understand what he was reading, much less my explanations.

"Wait here, citizen."

He left, and time stretched out eternally. I was afraid he would send me to the scanner room. That was where they stripped you and frisked you, put you in the middle of a metal V, in case you had pellets hidden in your stomach or, in your heart of hearts, felt like going to hell and taking everyone with you. I didn't have the first, but you could see the second all over me. Just the thought of it made me dizzy.

All my important things were tucked tightly in the back brace I was wearing. A poor alibi, but an alibi all the same. Pressed to my back and stomach I was carrying the euros still at my disposal, as well as Aurora Peralta's bank cards. In another hidden pocket I'd made in my purse, the cards and few documents that corresponded to my real identity were pressed tightly.

Things had to go terribly wrong for them to search me. But, of course, the person who decides how things pan out is not the one who's afraid, but the one who's inspiring fear. That was the thing; it was like playing with food before taking it to your mouth. Subdue the other's will without laying a finger on them.

The guy returned, taking long strides, his boredom weighing heavier than his boots.

"And what's your aunt's name then, citizen?"

"Francisca Peralta, Officer."

"Right, Francisca Peralta. Do you have any food with you?"

"No, Officer. You can confirm that."

"Hmmm . . . I say that because we have to watch for ecological and customs crimes."

My baggage was still open. The guard grabbed a book and smelled it.

"If you're a cook, why do you have no food with you?"

"Officer, I'm traveling to take care of a sick woman, not to cook."

"Hmmm. But what are these books about? Do they include recipes?"

"No, Officer, they're novels. I read them for pleasure."

"Hmmm . . . And where does your aunt live?"

"In Madrid, Officer."

"In what part of Madrid would that be, citizen?"

"In Las Ventas, Officer, near Plaza de Toros."

"Oh, really? They have bullfights in Madrid?"

I nodded.

"And what about you? Are you Spanish? If you're going for so long, it's because you're allowed to stay, is that right? You have papers?"

"My mother was Spanish and, as you can see, I'm a dual citizen."

"Hmmm . . . And where is the Spanish passport?"

My head spun and I got a sharp pain in my gut.

I took my hand to my pocket to remove it.

"Here it is."

"Why didn't you show me that before?"

"Well, Officer, because . . . because . . . I'm a citizen of this country, you know?" I said, my passport still in hand.

"Give it to me."

I hesitated a moment. If my life made any sense it was thanks to that document. I handed it to him with the feeling that I was giving up a kidney.

"Wait here."

He departed again. I got the impression that any situation that was marginally complex had to be run by someone higher up, as if his comprehension levels didn't extend to anything beyond the basic routines. Beside me waited a girl whose eight blocks of chocolate had been confiscated. She, who wasn't a Spanish national, explained hundreds of times that she was going to study for a masters in Barcelona. After nibbling on each of the blocks, the National Guard officer asked if she planned on coming back. Without hesitation, she said she did. Two tables beyond her, an older woman had to unravel balls of wool and explain it was for knitting. Almost every person waiting was a woman or elderly, a profile easy to intimidate.

I looked at the German shepherds that the guards used to detect drugs that came from other countries, which the officials concealed. The dogs didn't have muzzles and smelled everything, burying their snouts in crotches and people's handbags. The officers dug around, stuck their fingers where it would hurt us the most. They called us citizens but treated us like criminals.

They pretended to be suspicious of certain individuals, detaining them so that others who did have cocaine hidden on them could go through. It was profitable to turn a blind eye to the packages, to play for time with the rest of us. Drugs pay more than intimidation. And inspiring fear has its pleasures.

The National Guard officer came back, my passport in hand.

"Hmmm . . ."

I didn't understand what he meant by that noise. More than speak, he lowed.

"Come with me," he ordered.

I thought I was dead. I followed the man along gray corridors. I had no passport. No phone. No lifeline. I wasn't

Falcón or Peralta. If they raped me or made mincemeat of me, no one would find out. He led me to an office where an obese man was looking over some papers.

"Sit down. What is your name?"

"Aurora Peralta."

"Why are you going to Spain?"

"To take care of a sick family member."

"Are you carrying euros, citizen?"

I didn't know what his rank was, but, given that he seemed to be the one giving orders, I abandoned the idea of calling him "Officer."

"No, Commander."

"And how will you pay for your time there?"

"I'm staying with family."

The man inspected my passport and let out a sigh that sounded like he was passing wind.

"Corporal Gutiérrez tells me you're clean. To verify this, we'd have to put you through the scanner."

I must have opened my eyes as wide as plates.

"But don't worry, citizen, the state pays. It won't cost you a cent. In any case, it's time-consuming and we've got a full flight. Please do the favor of accompanying Corporal Gutiérrez; in the meantime, I'll hold on to your passport and, if you cooperate, we'll give it back."

Gutiérrez took his hands to his waist. I saw myself paying for a quick death with sex. What should I do? Scream? What for? How would that help?

"Whatever you say, Commander. If I can cooperate, I will," I responded, already swallowing semen.

"Go with the corporal . . . and do be sure to cooperate, citizen."

Gutiérrez accompanied me to the tarmac.

"Remove your vest," he ordered.

His familiarity frightened me. I took it off and left it on the table, beside my suitcase.

"Come up with me."

The plane was still parked, and I was still on the ground.

Corporate Gutiérrez walked with me down the corridors and concourse where passengers were wandering, headed for their departure gates. He stopped before one of the duty-free stores, that small empire of perfumes, liquor, and makeup. His tone changed suddenly.

"Look, mamita: you go in, you choose the Samsung television . . . that one over there, the biggest. You go to the cash register, show your papers, and come out here with it."

He spoke while I nodded.

"But Officer, I have no money to pay for it."

"Not to worry, m'hija. You just bring it over and that's it."

I chose the television, handed over my documents and flight details. The store employee printed a receipt and stapled it to the bag.

"Enjoy your purchase and have a safe journey," he said.

I went back to the official. He gestured at the floor with his nose and I placed the television there. An airport employee collected the bag. Only then did we embark on the walk back to the tarmac. We ended it where everything started:

standing before my baggage. I opened my suitcase again. He looked over it mechanically.

"Everything is in order, citizen," he said.

Only then did he give me back my passports, the Spanish and the Venezuelan, both in Aurora Peralta's name. The Spanish document came back to me accompanied by a yellow sticker in a circular shape. I went up the steps to the waiting lounge with difficulty. My legs were trembling.

In the glassed lounge of the departure gate, I looked out at the landing strip and the airport workers. Men and women who moved their arms as if in a bid to make the planes dance. The asphalt shone like a newly shined fork, while the turbines scraped at the windows with their snores. The clock in the corridor didn't work. Its dormant punctuality said two in the afternoon. I looked at my passport, flipping through its pages and trying to convince myself that, this time, I really was Aurora Peralta.

Around me, passengers were mesmerized by their phones. They killed time and quelled their anxiety by pressing their fingertips against the screens. The airport had turned into an air-conditioned crematory oven, in which someone—that woman, that boy, or that man with glasses—was sending out final missives before crossing the ocean, like someone rolling the last dice or—why not?—burning a boat behind them. Never coming back was the best thing that could happen to any of us.

My phone rang from inside my handbag. It was Ana. She screamed and broke down into crying spasms. I couldn't understand anything she was saying. Julio took the phone. Santiago was dead. They found him in a vacant lot on the outskirts of the city, three bullets in his head and a bag of cocaine in his backpack.

"Cocaine?"

"Yes, Adelaida. Haven't you seen the papers? The government has packaged the matter as only they know how. 'Murdered student leader of the resistance who trafficked drugs.'" There was interference on the line. "Can you hear me?"

"Yes, Julio. Put Ana on."

He told Ana to come to the phone.

"It's not true, you know that!"

"I know it's not. Listen to me. The important thing, Ana . . . the important thing is to calm down." I raised my voice, as if doing so would drive away my own surprise.

"No, no . . . !"

"Ana, listen to me!" It was impossible to talk to her. She wouldn't stop crying. "Ana, listen to me, Ana. Ana! Ana, can you hear me?"

The line went dead. I tried to call back several times, but it went straight to voice mail. I left three messages.

I clamped my eyes on the baggage vehicle parked next to the plane. The voice of an airline employee announced that boarding for flight 072x to Madrid was due to commence. The workers hastened to load the final boxes and pieces of luggage. Phone in hand, I looked at the suitcases, trying to make out mine, but didn't manage to identify it. All of them looked small, not large enough to hold the life of Aurora Peralta. The suitcases were treated like us: they were piled up and kicked about. We shared the same powerlessness, like we were all in a giant fish market. Someone was quartering us, opening us up, and shamelessly rummaging around to find what we were carrying within.

That day, I understood what certain good-byes are made of. Mine, from that fist of shit and viscera, that disappearing coastline, the country I couldn't shed even a single tear over.

I got on the plane and found my seat. I turned off my phone and, with it, my nerves. I looked out the window. It was night, and electric currents of misery and beauty were shooting through the city. Caracas looked welcoming and at the same time terrible, the hot nest of an animal that still peered at me with fierce snake eyes in the darkness.

Only a small difference in sound separates "leave" from "live."

I WENT TO THE RIVER to wash the sheets. A girl dressed in torn pants was by my side. A gash encrusted with blood showed through a hole in the fabric above her right knee. I looked at the washbowl full of dirty rags. I asked the girl her name, what happened to her, where her mother was. She grabbed my hand and pulled me with the strength of a Cyclops. We went under, down into dirty water that didn't seem at all like the clean and calm water's edge where I'd rung out my linens. We floated among snakes of excrement, which moved slowly alongside dead horses and riders. Their eyes were open, the color of cooked yolks: sockets emptied of life. As we swam clumsily in the warm soup of blood and shit, the bodies of beasts and men collided with us. Unable to turn around, we went on beneath the current, which spun us in nightmarish slow motion. The girl pulled my hand and pulled me under, farther still, down among the algae and the tendrils of firm, hardened shit.

I wanted to swim to the surface, but the girl tugged my hand again, showing me something. Behind a saddled, rider-less horse a curled-up body was floating. A fetal man in a septic placenta. The girl swam to him, not letting me go.

Holding him by the shoulder, she turned his body so we could see his face. It was Santiago. The little girl used her free arm to reach around him. The three of us embraced, the shoal of beasts, dung, and dead men surrounding us.

When I opened my eyes, a flight attendant had a hand on my shoulder.

"Are you okay?"

I must have cried out.

"Yes, I'm fine."

My mouth was claggy, thick. I'd been holding my handbag on my lap the whole time.

"We will be landing at Barajas Airport in an hour. Would you like breakfast?"

I nodded, dazed. A sweet smell of baked bread impregnated the air. The woman sat a tray of food in front of me: cubes of fruit, cold butter, and a limp omelet for unhungry travelers.

"Would you like tea? Coffee? Creamer? Sugar or sweetener?"

Too many questions. Would you like to proceed or return? Is your name Adelaida Falcón or Aurora Peralta? Did you kill her or was she already dead? Are you fleeing or stealing? The plane seemed small, suffocating.

"I'm thirsty," I said.

"Would you like some water? Juice? Pineapple or orange?"

"Orange, I want orange."

I gulped down the concentrate. Life and presence of mind returned to me with the chemical taste of that citrus, irrigating my parched brain. I scanned my surroundings. No one was seated by my side. I played with a bread roll. I glanced at the minuscule tubs. Everything had come to an end in the same way it had begun: with a pile of completely useless plates. I turned to the window, the black sky an idle threat, as if the slow rising of the sun would pull up the day that was ending on the other side of the ocean. To leave everything behind: the marvel that the Atlantic confers on those who cross it.

I barely ate. The flight attendant took the tray and hurried to collect the crumpled napkins and empty cup. Flight 072x's captain announced that in twenty minutes we would land at Madrid–Barajas Airport. The temperature was twenty-one degrees Celsius. I turned my face to the frozen window again. Cities have such a surreal look when you gaze on them from the air: as if they were false, like miniatures or models. Highways, houses, plots of land, pools, tiny cars, drivers headed who knows where. Small lives, insignificant, far off. We landed suddenly. The plane careened along the runway. The smell of cold bread followed me to the only door, which birthed us passengers one by one. The seats looked like a battleground: forgotten pillows, crumpled paper, wounded paper cups cradling the remains of juices and sodas, people's last yawns fogged on the windows.

I moved along the jet bridge, passport in hand, clutching my ID like a compass. The airport had a rich-country modernity about it. On arriving at immigration, I found two lines. I stood in the line for Europeans, as if I were secreting stolen goods in my carry-on baggage. I awaited my turn. A National Police officer inspected my passport. His face was clean-shaven, and he was fine-looking. He could never be as dangerous as Corporal Gutiérrez in his soldier's uniform clustered with medals.

The process of becoming someone else gets complicated when there's a counter in the way. It's like selling anguish by the pound. The Spanish passport, my passport, didn't have a single stamp on its pages. They were completely blank. That must have caught the officer's attention, because he took his time examining each page. He looked at the date of issue and my photograph as Aurora Peralta, closed it, and handed it back to me. Good-bye; nothing else. In that small room, by the deed and grace of that stamped paper, I was Spanish. Perhaps for the first and only time, I was the person I was supposed to be supplanting.

I moved forward, my legs weak. I passed through the airport concourse, holding up my name as if it would light my way. When I arrived at the baggage hall, the conveyor belts spat out cases. The fluorescent lights made the room seem like an incubator where the woman housed inside me could grow. I was my own mother and my own child. The deed and grace of a desperate act. That day, I gave birth to myself. I delivered myself, clenching my teeth, not looking back. My suitcase was the final strain. I grabbed it by the handgrip and headed for the exit.

"Fucking country: you'll never see me again," I said under my breath.

That morning, for once in my life, I won. A harpoon had pierced my side, but I won.

Every sea is an operating room and a sharp scalpel slices into those who dare cross it.

A FAMILY WAS WAITING, balloons and banners in
hand. At first, they seemed euphoric; a few seconds
later disappointment overcame them as they realized the person they were expecting wasn't among those coming through
the glass doors. A few men were holding up electronic tablets
that displayed the name of a passenger, and overly made-up
women dressed as flight attendants were awaiting groups of
tourists. I wanted to hit all of them. I don't know why, but I
wanted to do damage, hurt, destroy. Wanted to be a hurricane. A force of nature. I pulled my suitcase after me until I
arrived at a free bench.

I checked the address: Number 8, Calle Londres, Las Ventas. "You have to tell the driver that the address is inside the
M-30 ring road," María José had written in her last email.
Ten lines with instructions, and, after that, she wished me
bon voyage. But what did that mean, after everything? Who
gets wished such a thing? The one returning, or the one leaving? The person you are when you're leaving, or the person
you are when you arrive as someone else?

What would happen if I didn't show up, if I got lost in
Madrid and made a life for myself without first checking

in with a family I didn't know? Why did I have to implant myself among people I knew nothing about when I could, with my new surname, disappear without explanation? I felt afraid, much more afraid than when I disposed of the body of the woman who had now gifted me her name.

I looked at my shoes, the only things of my own that I was wearing. Anyone would have thought I was from the provinces and had never been on a plane or used an ATM. The patterned, voluminous clothing was a dead giveaway for my impersonation. Since I had started being Aurora Peralta—dressing and acting like her, remembering and even sometimes thinking like her—I perceived myself as an undesirable woman, bewildered and unremarkable.

Where does a lie start? In a name? A gesture? A memory? Maybe a word?

Giving voice to Aurora Peralta called for dissolving her inside me, assimilating her until I resembled the remote idea of her that I had in my head. Being Aurora Peralta initiated a battle with myself. Ceasing to be. Forfeiting existence, surrendering to her version, which in the next few days would have to take shape in my voice, my memories, in the way I reacted and desired, in my appearance. How would I fill up the first meeting, the first days, the chitchat that follows the basic instructions of here is the bathroom, the coffee machine works like this, here's how you turn on the TV? What fuel would burn in the moments that followed the truce of courtesy, the welcome to the stranger? I could lament the death of a mother who wasn't mine, but what could I tell them about her sickness and demise? Sooner or later the topic would come up. What expression should I wear when one of them referred to the house, the one they went on about, Julia Peralta as much as Paquita, in the letters sent in the last years?

Two days before my trip I opened the letter from Spanish Social Security addressed to Julia Peralta. It was dated recently, and in it was a request to send proof that she was still living, to guarantee her widow's payment. Six letters of the same type had been filed, one per year since the death of Julia Peralta. They were together with an apostilled document in which Aurora Peralta testified before the Spanish consulate that her mother was still living, but that her health problems prevented her from coming in person. A medical certificate, signed by the same official, served as evidence. There had been no time for Aurora Peralta to answer the last letter; and though I'd taken the precaution of obtaining a similar document for an absurd sum, I didn't dare send it.

"Mamá always says I'm gaining weight," Aurora Peralta had noted in the earliest entry of a diary I found in the nightstand drawer. It was hidden away, as if she were keeping it from prying eyes. It was a blue notebook, its pages yellowing like a sheet stained with urine. It was full of straightforward musings: sketches of an adolescent who burned with resentment as youth neared its end, and then who ended up shutting down in resignation in adulthood. With one line for every day lived, Aurora Peralta could have reached eighty years and the notebook would still have blank pages.

"Today I'm sad." "Yesterday I didn't eat dinner." "I don't want to go to the restaurant. Mamá is ranting." "I'm getting fat again." "Mamá's mood is intolerable." "Today I went to bingo." "I don't want to speak to anyone." "I hate it when Mamá berates me." "Mamá wanted to go out today, I didn't. We fought."

More than feelings, Aurora Peralta overturned the inventory of someone who seemed to plod along regardless. On a few occasions she alluded to something that extended beyond the universe of her own health; the fights with her mother; or the restaurant, where she was needed more and more.

"I don't like that place." "I don't want to be there." "Cooking is boring."

The jottings of the last years drew an even blurrier picture of who Aurora Peralta was or what she wanted. The only clear thing was that she didn't like the eatery, much less working with her mother. "Today I had to fry eighty empanadas." "Mamá will go to cook at the party headquarters. I don't want to go. I'm no servant." Descriptions of barely two or three lines, endowed with an ancillary contempt for how her mother earned a living. Her boredom was much greater than the feelings of rejection the business evoked in her.

Julia Peralta's sickness, which Aurora described only as cancer, took on in her diary the form of a person. An individual with a will. Something like a new family member who moved in and to whom she attributed moods. Everything was written in a brittle way, almost theatrical, like a child playing with two cans of soda, mimicking the voices of inanimate objects.

"Today cancer treated my mother badly, it's left her lying in bed. I opened and closed the restaurant; no good." "Cancer behaved better, Mamá got out of bed today." "Cancer was brutal today, we couldn't open. At the clinic all day, I feel sorry for Mamá. But she brought this on herself, bent over the stove all day. The one good thing was not having to fry."

Few objects stood out among the belongings of Aurora's that I found in her bedroom. She didn't seem to read much. On the shelf she had few books, at most two or three novels by Isabel Allende and a copy of *Doña Bárbara*, the national classic. She didn't seem to listen to music, either. She did like cutting out newspaper clippings. She had mismatched collections. A recipe for *tocinillo de cielo*, rice pudding, and profiteroles together with the daily recap of the telenovelas showing on TV. I could reconstruct the story arc of an entire decade with her article collection. Aurora must have suffered at each episode's ending, because she used a pen to underline the summaries. Endings that, though they always seemed the same to me, she highlighted as exceptional.

On reaching the third folder of clippings, I turned to stone. Aurora Peralta had kept a copy of the picture of the soldier dead on the pavement, the same one I discovered the day of my tenth birthday and kept a long time. I unfolded the front page to look at the image of the boy whose eyebrows were sodden with blood. The newspaper layout made me realize soon enough why Aurora had kept the picture: it belonged to the same sheet, the one printed with both the first and last page, as the TV reviews. At the opposite extreme of the newspaper edition that reported on the first bout of social unrest the both of us experienced, was—duly underlined—the obituary of the actress Doris Wells, known for *La Fiera*. Wells was our dream witch, the elegant villain, the one who brought others to their knees with her harsh eyebrows and head of golden hair. I held on to the death of a country, and Aurora, to the death of a telenovela actress. Both were a fiction.

I felt dazed, leaden, incapable of dragging my baggage to the airport doors. When I looked up, I saw groups of people going through the same motions. Anxious families whose faces changed: smiles at the passenger who might be—this time really might be—the one they were waiting for, suddenly wiped from their faces with the disappointing realization that, ah, no, it wasn't. But look, look, that's him! Scattered around the edges of the crowd, the same men wielding tablets, though really they were different men. Women, overly made up as they'd been earlier, but different individuals, greeting a different group of Japanese tourists. Everything was both the same and different, like a lamp turned on and off. And there I was, seated on the same bench, not moving a muscle, and wondering what to do about my masterstroke, as if it were a grenade.

The transfusions from Aurora Peralta that ran through my veins weren't sufficient. To make them work, I'd have to drain all my blood. I had to get my act together. Aurora Peralta had been unlucky, but that didn't mean I had to be. I hadn't come so far only to founder.

I made my way to the taxi rank.

"To Calle Londres, number eight, please," I said to the driver after pulling the door shut.

The white sedan took off in a hurry and merged onto the M-30 ring road as a male voice told us the time over the radio: "It's nine a.m., eight a.m. in the Canary Islands."

We crossed a huge highway that had glass buildings on either side. The sky looked as clean as a window. I went over what I knew about my new family. María José worked as a nurse in a municipal health center. After her divorce, she and her son moved to a rental apartment a few blocks from Francisca's house. It was a fifth-floor apartment that overlooked the street, well lit. "You'll like it," she'd stated in her last email. Francisca, her mother, was living in the old family house, between Calle Cardenal Belluga and Calle Julio Camba, very close to Plaza América Española, a place I learned to love thanks to the three olive trees that never changed, the only constant in a life of four seasons. Francisca lived alone, but a Bolivian woman took care of her. Francisca's lucidity, I understood, came and went. "You'll see her," wrote María José. "Yes, I'll see her," I said to myself under my breath as the buildings left me speechless. Each of them taller and more modern than the one before.

The taxi turned right on Ventas bridge and crossed behind the Plaza de Toros, a place where bulls and men met their deaths: the same liturgy as my city, celebrated opera-style. Paying for a seat to watch death play out. Why would I, when in my country I could do so free of charge?

Number eight on Calle Londres seemed a nice building. The door was open. A man with leathery, wrinkled skin was sweeping steps that looked impeccable to me. He was wearing navy-blue overalls and had a smoker's smile, his teeth marred with dark spots. He set the broom aside and helped me with my baggage.

"I'm going to the fifth floor."

"Oh, okay . . . to María José's. She said she was expecting someone. Do you want me to go with you?"

"No, thank you," I said.

When the elevator doors met, I looked at myself in the mirror. I looked terrible. I was worn out, aged, bitter. Between the woman I was and the one returning my gaze was a long line of specters, washed-out versions of an original document. I'd lost a lot of weight. I looked older, old-fashioned, as if instead of coming from another country I was arriving from another time. That was how Aurora Peralta's mother must have looked when she arrived in my city. But I was alive. She no longer was.

Living: a miracle that I still don't understand fully, one that grabs hold with the teeth of guilt. Surviving is part of the horror that travels with anyone who escapes. A plague that strives to bring us down when we're healthy, to remind us that someone else was more deserving of staying alive.

I halted before a wooden door identified with the letter *D*. I straightened and pressed the buzzer. I heard a few steps and the creaking of the lock.

"You are . . ."

"It's me, Aurora."

It was ten thirty in the morning. Nine thirty in the Canary Islands.

In Caracas, it would always be night.

ACKNOWLEDGMENTS

To my sister Cristina, the poet who taught me to read inside myself and lived each of these pages as if they were her own.

To my mother, for her truth.

To my father, the *Gran Gran Capitán*.

To my brother Juan Carlos, for showing me that an ocean existed, and that I could cross it whenever I wanted.

To my brother Carlos José, for his disconcerting smile in the middle of the storm.

To María Aponte Borgo, the one and only writer.

To José and Eulalia Sainz. Now I understand you.

To my women: those who write and those who don't.

To Óscar: without you, no novel would exist. Not this one, not all those in the bottom drawer.

To Emilio, for the push toward *La Carretera*.

To Marina Penalva, for knowing how to read this story deeply. And, above all, for believing in it.

To Haydn, Mahler, Verdi, and Callas.

To the cantos del pilón I heard from Soledad Bravo, the drums from San Juan, and the polo margariteño, "La embarazada del viento."

To my land, always broken. Scattered across both sides of the ocean.

A NOTE FROM THE TRANSLATOR

In recreating this work in English, I've paid close attention to the rhythm and shades of Adelaida's voice, which vary greatly depending on her state of mind. In the beginning, her voice has a staccato quality, her utterances truncated by grief; later, that voice is all energetic resilience, fueled by her determination to survive. Perhaps the sentence I spent the most time reworking was *"Tan solo una letra separa «partir» de «parir»."* (Just a single letter separates "to leave" from "to give birth.") In the novel, Adelaida describes the act of adopting a new identity as giving birth to a new self. Birth is given special metaphorical weight, recurring as it does in key scenes that include her recollections of her mother, her realization that she herself will never be one, and her removing Aurora's body from the building. Yet meaning resides as much in the linguistic structure as it does in the message content, and to translate *"partir"* as "to leave" and *"parir"* as "to give birth" would mean to lose the linguistic similarity. How, then, to get the meaning—all of it—across? After much wrestling with myself, I finally decided on "Only a small difference in sound separates 'leave' from 'live.'" If she wants to live, Adelaida must leave Venezuela, and her old self, behind.

—Elizabeth Bryer

Here ends Karina Sainz Borgo's
It Would Be Night in Caracas.

The first edition of this book was printed and
bound at LSC Communications in
Harrisonburg, Virginia, September 2019.

A NOTE ON THE TYPE

The text of this novel was set in Sabon, a typeface created by Jan Tschichold—a German-born typographer and book designer—over a three-year period in the 1960s. A group of German printers approached Tschichold to design a font using the elegant and highly legible types created by 16th century Parisian publisher Claude Garamond that would look the same whether set by hand or machine. What resulted was Sabon, a font that has remained popular for its smooth and clean look.

HARPERVIA

An imprint dedicated to publishing international voices,
offering readers a chance to encounter other lives and
other points of view via the language of the imagination.